"Is he Prince Charming?"

The preschooler asked, pointing toward the door.

Ali's gaze followed the little finger to the doorway, and she blinked in surprise.

If Prince Charming existed outside the pages of a storybook, surely the man at the door was the genuine article. His broad shoulders filled the doorframe, and for a moment, the sight of him made her forget to breathe . . .

On closer look, he bore only a passing resemblance to a hero in a children's tale. His dark good looks held a provocative edge that brought to mind a black knight of an erotic bedtime story only a woman could appreciate.

"Sorry to interrupt, but there wasn't anyone at the receptionist's desk." His velvet-smooth voice sent a tingle through her.

"Miss Ali, is he my Prince Charming?" Tiffany asked again, more insistently.

No, he's all mine.

Operation Prince Charming

PHYLLIS BOURNE

Montlake
Romance

Published by Montlake Romance
P.O. Box 400818
Las Vegas, NV 89140

ISBN-13: 9781477806647
ISBN-10: 1477806644

For my beauty and fashion blogging sisters:

The Product Junkie Diva, Beautylogic, Make-up By RenRen, Clumps of Mascara, Mischo Beauty, Yummy411, Kwana Writes, Soul Pretty, Brown Girl Gumbo, Calming Corners, Karen-Of A Certain Age, Pumps and Gloss, The Home Spa Goddess, La Bella Figura, The Best Joyce, MissWhoEverYouAre, Middle Rageously, The Anti-Hair Slave/Beauty Blvd, Black Vixen Beauty, Coup de Coeur, Inverted Reflection, That's Not My Age, Once Upon A Fashionista, My Wardrobe Today, Sweet Tea In Seattle and Chelle at Hanging by a Thin Thread. You ladies make the web and my life beautiful!

And as always, for Byron

Operation Prince Charming

Chapter One

Hunter Coleman leaned back on his elbows and watched her scramble around the opulent bedroom, gathering up the clothes she'd eagerly stripped off for him just hours ago.

"I told you this would have to be a quickie." She balanced her lithe body on a stiletto heel as she hurriedly slipped on the other. "Now I'm running late, and it's all your fault."

"My fault?" Hunter pushed himself upright on the bed and grinned at his girlfriend of the past two years. "I'm not the one who wanted to break out the handcuffs."

Ignoring him, Erica surveyed her appearance in the gilt-edge mirror and frowned. "I spent hours getting this hair sewn in yesterday. Now look at it." She threw her expertly manicured hands in the air. "What's Vivian Cox going to think if I show up at her luncheon looking like this?"

Hunter took in the disheveled mane, whisker-scorched cheeks, and lipstick smudged by his kisses. Despite the scowl marring her beautiful, walnut-hued face, she looked like a woman who'd spent a long, satisfying morning in bed.

"She'll wonder why you stopped what you were doing to waste the afternoon kissing her a—"

"Hunter!" She cut him off. "Must you be so crude?"

She grabbed a silver brush from her vanity and began attacking the mass of tangles. "Can't you even make an attempt to like my new friends?"

"Friends?" Hunter couldn't hold back the sarcasm tainting his query.

"Well . . ." she stammered, brushing her faux tresses harder. "I might be closer to being accepted by them if you didn't act so uncouth."

Uncouth? He watched her pull bobby pins from between her lips and strategically jab them into hanks of hair. What was he supposed to do, nod politely as those snobs pelted her with their thinly veiled insults?

"What's wrong with your old friends?" *The ones who actually give a damn about you,* he wanted to add, but thought better of it.

Erica smoothed her hair, which she'd finally managed to wrestle into a prim bun. "They can't get me into the Ladies' Lunch League or the Highland Oaks Country Club."

"Then maybe you don't belong there either."

Her jaw tightened, making Hunter wish he'd kept his trap shut. "I belong there *now*," she said, pausing to put on a pair of golf-ball-sized diamond studs. "Vivian is a fixture on the Nashville social circuit. One word from her and I'm in. So I'll do whatever it takes to get on her good side."

Hunter groaned and collapsed back onto the feather pillows. After pissing the night away on a stakeout that hadn't gotten him any closer to finding the people responsible for burglarizing over thirty homes in his precinct, spending the morning with a naked Erica beneath him had been a pleasant diversion. He didn't want it to deteriorate into a now familiar argument.

"Look, Erica, I know this socialite thing is a big deal to you, but is it worth alienating the people who were there for you before the money?"

She turned away from the mirror and fastened him with a contact-enhanced, hazel-eyed stare. "I've outgrown them."

Hunter shook his head, feeling the intimacy of their morning tryst as well as their once solid relationship slipping away. He stared at the woman preening in the mirror as she brushed another layer of powder across her cheekbones.

Six months ago, he'd been on the verge of proposing to the private-duty nurse. Then her longtime employer died and left her that damned money. Since then she'd dedicated herself to reaching the top of the city's social ladder, and she apparently didn't care who she had to step on to move up a rung.

"Have you outgrown me too?" he asked carefully. "Is that why I haven't heard from you in two weeks?"

Tossing back the covers, he swung his legs over the side of her canopied bed and grabbed his pants from the floor. He was beat. She was annoyed. It was best he got dressed and headed home.

"Of course not." Erica abandoned the mirror, and Hunter felt her arms slip around his waist. She pressed a kiss to his back. "You know better."

"Do I?" He spun around and stared into her eyes, wishing he could remove the tinted lenses and once again see the warm brown gaze of the woman beneath the layers of makeup and diamonds. The woman he hoped would soon return to her senses once the excitement of her new-found wealth wore off.

"So what if I dumped some deadweight?"

Hunter winced at her characterization of the longtime relationships that once sustained her.

"It doesn't change how I feel about you. I love you." Erica's gaze drifted to the rumpled bed. "Didn't I show you just how much all morning?"

He heaved a sigh, releasing the tension trapped between his shoulder blades. Maybe he was being too hard on her. They'd both been busy lately. A spike in burglary cases had him putting in long hours on the job, and Erica had been equally occupied trying to break into the tight-knit country club set.

They just needed to spend more time together, he thought. And for Erica to work this nonsense out of her system.

Hunter hauled her against him. Her sharp hipbones dug into his skin, and again, he noted how thin she'd grown. The first few pounds she'd dieted off her nearly six-foot frame had given her the ultralean look of a fashion model.

Now she just looked and felt painfully skinny.

"Well?" Erica asked.

"How about you show me again tonight after we play poker with Pete and Sandy?"

"Poker? That was tonight?"

"Yeah, Pete says Sandy's been out for revenge ever since she lost her pedicure money to him last time," Hunter chuckled. "He claims he's going to let her win tonight because her feet are like sandpaper, but don't tell her he said that."

Erica averted her eyes. "Um . . . uh . . . Hunter. Honey, I already have plans for this evening."

His arms dropped to his sides as he looked at her, not believing she was pulling this on him again. "We can't bail on them again. We canceled last week because of some party. Besides, they've already booked a babysitter."

"It wasn't a party, it was a wine tasting," she clarified, as if it would make a difference.

"So what's tonight's excuse?"

"An exhibit for an emerging artist. He's all the rage with the elite . . ."

Hunter frowned, and she stopped midsentence. She reached out to him, but he stepped away and shrugged into his shirt.

"Cut the bullshit, Erica. This is me. Since when do you care about art?" he said. "Up until a few months ago, your only piece of art was an oil painting of Prince wearing purple butt-out pants."

Hunter glanced around the lavishly decorated bedroom. Like with her astronomically priced penthouse, designer wardrobe, and personal sushi chef, Erica's interest in art was simply something else she hoped would impress the town's socialites enough to gain entry into their rich bitch clique.

"I forgot about poker night. I'm sorry," she said hurriedly. "But I'm one of the exhibit's sponsors. I have to be there."

"Whatever," Hunter managed to get out through his clenched teeth. Talking to her lately had been like talking to a brick wall, one he was tired of beating his head against.

"Come on, don't be mad. How about I take everyone out to dinner next week? I'll hire a nanny for Pete and Sandy's boys and have Tanaka do the cooking? Just pick a night."

"No, thanks." Hunter stuffed his wallet into his back pocket and grabbed his keys. He could just imagine what Pete, his best friend and fellow detective, would think of sitting down to a plate of Erica's sushi chef's rice and raw fish. "If you change your mind, I'll be with our friends."

"You could always come to the exhibit with me," she said hesitantly.

He raised an eyebrow. The last time he'd accompanied Erica to one of those highbrow functions, it had been a complete disaster. He'd sat in silence while their dinner companions tried to top each other with endless boasts about their latest high-priced acquisition, dozing off somewhere between the DuBois' beauty of a sailboat docked in Palm Beach and the Cortlands' new twin-engine Cessna.

A furious Erica had awakened him with an elbow to his rib cage.

"You're joking about my coming along with you, right?" he asked.

Erica's lips firmed into a line.

"That's what I thought," Hunter said.

He turned to leave, but she clamped a hand on his arm. "Don't you dare try to make me the bad guy here," she said.

"What?" Hunter spun around, wondering how she could utter those words with a straight face.

"How many times have you bailed on me at the last minute because of some robbery across town or those stupid burglaries?"

She wouldn't think they were so stupid if she

were the victim, he thought, but he refused to get into a side disagreement with her on top of the one they were already having.

"Oh, come on, you can hardly compare the situations. I've only broken a date when something—"

"Important came up," she finished.

"Exactly," Hunter said.

"I never nagged you about work because I've always understood how important your job is to you," Erica said, anchoring a fist on her bony hip. "How come I don't get the same consideration about something significant to me?"

This time it was Hunter who fell silent. Not once could he remember her complaining when he ran out in the middle of one of their dates.

"I deserve better from you," she said softly.

Hunter opened his mouth to argue, but guilt slammed it shut. She was right. He wasn't being fair, and she had a right to expect more from him.

He blew out a weary sigh. "What do you want me to do?"

Erica flashed a victorious smile as she retrieved a cream-colored envelope from the nightstand and handed it to him. "After our last outing, my new publicist suggested this and I think it's a fabulous idea."

He broke the gold seal on the back of the envelope and pulled out an embossed card.

"A *Manners Makeover* at the Spencer School of Etiquette?" he read aloud. His gut clenched as if he were bracing for a punch. The urge to tell her exactly what he thought of the idea, her publicist, and the Spencer School of Etiquette bubbled up, but he managed to squelch it.

He glared at the paper in his hand for a long time, before releasing a long sigh. "Okay, when do we start?"

"Don't be silly. The lessons aren't for us." Erica spoke slowly as if he were new to the English language. *"They're for you."*

Ali Spencer donned the Polite Princess hand puppet for a quick review of the manners lesson she'd given the four-year-olds in her Perfectly Polite Tea Party class.

"So again, fellow princesses, what do we do if we're having dinner at a restaurant and accidently drop our fork on the floor?" Ali asked, using her hand to move the puppet's mouth.

"I know! I know!" Samantha, the only girl in the class not dressed in a ruffled or embroidered dress, stuck her hand in the air.

Ali smiled at the jeans-clad tomboy and nodded encouragingly.

"Pick it up and lick it clean!" Samantha shouted, her cheeks bulging with the sugar cookies she'd grabbed off her pink place setting and jammed into her mouth.

"Nooooo." The little girl seated next to Samantha rolled her eyes skyward. "You leave it and ask for a new one."

"That's right, Tiffany," Ali said, through the princess hand puppet.

Having already issued several gentle reminders to Samantha about talking with her mouth full, Ali moved on. The child stood out enough from the other girls, and she didn't want to keep singling her out.

"Now, what do you do if there's something on your plate you don't like?"

A beaming Tiffany raised her hand, and Ali bobbed the plush puppet's head. "Go ahead, Tiffany."

"Is *he* Prince Charming?" the preschooler asked, pointing toward the door.

Ali's gaze followed the little finger to the doorway, and she blinked in surprise.

If Prince Charming existed outside the pages of a storybook, surely the man at the door was the genuine article. His broad shoulders filled the door frame, and for a moment the sight of him made her forget to breathe.

No, she silently corrected.

On closer look, he bore only a passing resemblance to a hero in a children's tale. His dark good looks held a provocative edge that brought to mind a black knight of an erotic, bedtime story only a grown woman could appreciate.

"Sorry to interrupt, but there wasn't anyone

at the receptionist's desk." His velvet-smooth voice sent a tingle through her.

"Miss Ali, is he my Prince Charming?" Tiffany asked again, more insistently.

No, he's all mine.

The words leapt into Ali's head out of nowhere, and she suddenly realized she was experiencing something she hadn't felt since before her divorce.

Pure. Sexual. Attraction.

He was tall, the top of his head nearly touching the top of the door frame, with skin the color of iced mocha. Her eyes skimmed over his blue polo shirt, taking in the way it molded against his muscular chest and flat abs.

"Miss Ali?"

A tug at the hem of her dress roused Ali from her lust-induced stupor and reminded her she was supposed to be teaching manners to a roomful of girls riding a sugar cookie buzz.

She cleared her throat as if the gesture would simultaneously clear her head and looked down at Tiffany's hopeful face.

"He's not a prince, honey," she said.

There was no such thing as Prince Charming, Ali thought. She'd learned that bitter lesson the hard way.

Tiffany's pigtails bounced as she looked from her prince to Ali and back again. She gave Ali one last skeptical glance before rejoining the other girls.

This man was like a hot fudge sundae, Ali thought, preparing to address him. Sure, it looked delicious, but indulging meant moments of euphoria followed by regret.

She pulled the princess puppet off her hand and walked to the door. "How can I help you?"

"I have an appointment with Miss Spencer."

Realization dawned on her. "Oh, you must be Detective Coleman. I'm sorry. I meant to call you this morning and reschedule," she said. "My aunt was supposed to meet with you, but she had an emergency."

A look of pure relief fell over his face, and his big body visibly relaxed. "Well, that's that." He shrugged. "Thanks anyway."

Ali didn't have to be a rocket scientist to deduce the hunk was making a break for it. Odds were if she let him leave now, he wouldn't return. While there was nothing she'd like more than putting some distance between herself and the man who'd just reawakened her sex drive, the floundering school needed the generous check the Chanel-clad woman had given Aunt Rachel for his classes.

"Hold on a moment." Ali glanced at the clock on the wall. "The children's parents will be here to pick them up in a few minutes. Would you mind waiting in my office?"

Girlish shrieks erupted, and he ran past her. His big, surprisingly agile, body crossed the room in three long strides. Ali spun around to discover, in the few minutes she'd turned away, Samantha had used a chair to help scale an eight-foot bookcase and was now dangling from the top by one arm.

"I'm a mountain climber," Samantha squealed.

Ali watched in horror as the little girl lost her grip and fell backward. "Oh my God!" she gasped, charging toward her.

In what seemed like slow motion, the man extended his arms and a laughing Samantha fell into them, seconds before she would have slammed onto the hardwood floor.

"You okay, kiddo?" He set the child back on her feet.

"Yeah!" Samantha said. "Wanna catch me again?"

"I think you'd better save your climbing for the monkey bars. You don't want to give me or your teacher here a heart attack."

Still shaking, Ali recovered enough to snatch Samantha into a hug. "You scared me." Ali gave the little girl a tight squeeze.

"Hey! Those are my cookies," Samantha yelled over Ali's shoulder at another child, oblivious of the near miss. She squirmed and Ali reluctantly released her.

"I told you he was Prince Charming," Tiffany said. Hero worship shone in her eyes as she looked up at the detective.

Ali followed her gaze and for a split second wished she could indulge the same childlike belief, but her ex had forever tainted any romantic fantasies of handsome princes or happily-ever-after.

"Seems you have your hands full," Detective Coleman said, moving in the direction of the door. "I'll just let you get back to work."

Oh, no, you don't.

Ali had no intention of letting him get away or returning the fat payment for his classes already deposited in the school's account.

She spotted some of the girls' mothers walking through the door.

"My office is the second on the left, Detective," she said pointedly.

The corner of his mouth tugged upward in the hint of a smile.

"Wow! Who was that?" Tiffany's mother asked, practically drooling as he walked past her.

"My next appointment," Ali said.

The mom beside her raised an eyebrow. "Lucky you."

Lucky? Ali nearly laughed aloud.

In her experience, fine men didn't bring luck. All they'd ever brought her was trouble.

What in the hell are you doing here?

Hunter dropped into a chair in Alison Spencer's office.

"Trying to keep your relationship from going up in smoke," he muttered, ignoring the tiny voice inside him whispering it might already be too late.

Lingering irritation from the other morning sparked up in him, but he mentally extinguished it. Erica's good sense would eventually return.

Clinging to the memories of the old Erica, his Erica, was the only way he could justify returning to the Spencer School of Etiquette, almost three decades after he and his brother had been kicked out.

He'd braced himself for the unpleasant task of facing the strict, no-nonsense woman who'd run the school for as long as he could remember, but luckily she hadn't been there.

Unfortunately, his chance to escape had been thwarted.

Resigned to his fate, he glanced around the office. Sunshine streamed through windows so clean they practically sparkled, bathing the small space in light. The office, as well as the rest of the old building, was immaculate. The worn hardwood floors gleamed, and the faint scent of lemon cleanser tinged the air.

His eyes roamed over a shelf of books behind an antique, polished wood desk. Several bearing Alison Spencer's name on the spine caught his eye. His curiosity aroused, he walked over and plucked one from the shelf.

"Manners Count," he murmured.

He flipped it over and a photograph of the woman he'd just met smiled serenely at him from the back cover. Her hair fell in glossy curls around her shoulders, and a string of pearls encircled her neck. She wore a sweater in a shade of pink so bright it seemed blinding. However, something about the rich, honey tones of her caramel skin made it work for her.

Hunter skimmed the short bio beneath the photo.

Author and south Florida lifestyle columnist, he read, and wondered what had brought her to Tennessee. He shrugged as he placed the book back on the shelf and picked up the one beside it.

"Manners Count II: Turning Men into Gentlemen." He read the title aloud and began thumbing through it. He stopped at a chapter on television protocol. The words *relinquish* and *remote control* jumped out at him, along with the phrase *turn off the sports channel*.

Hunter snapped the book shut and took another look at Alison Spencer's likeness on the cover jacket. "How am I going to get through three weeks of this shit?"

"Sounds like we have our work cut out for us, don't we?" a feminine voice said from behind him.

Aww, hell, Hunter groaned inwardly. He turned around slowly still holding the book in his hand. Alison Spencer stood behind him with her arms crossed over her chest. Her pink-tinted lips were turned down in a frown.

If he hadn't been so embarrassed, he would have laughed aloud. It was hard to take the disapproval of a woman who reminded him of sugary sweet cotton candy seriously.

She stood at least a foot shorter than his six foot three inches and wore a dress so pink it looked as if she'd been splashed with a bottle of Pepto-Bismol. Her hair was tied off her perfect oval face with a ribbon the same obnoxious shade of pink, which made the fresh-faced Alison Spencer look more like one of her pint-sized students than a teacher.

His gaze followed her to her desk. It was then he noticed the bright yellow pelicans dotted all over her dress and the killer curves she hid beneath it.

Despite her petite stature, this was no girl.

Alison Spencer was all woman.

"I didn't hear you come in," he said finally.

"Obviously."

He returned the book to the shelf, nearly brushing her as she retrieved a folder from her desk. He caught the scent of her perfume, a light citrusy mix that brought to mind sliced limes and oranges.

"Thanks for waiting," she said, then paused. "And thank you for coming to Samantha's rescue back there."

"No problem," he replied, glad the attention

had veered away from his blunder. "Besides, seems like that one would be happier playing T-ball than tea party."

She sighed. "You're probably right." She seated herself behind her desk and gestured for him to take the chair in front of it. "Unfortunately for her, she's the daughter her parents kept trying for after five sons."

Hunter nodded his understanding.

"Her mom's hoping my class, and interacting with other girls her age, will generate some interest in . . ." She hesitated as if searching for the right word.

"Sugar, spice, and everything nice," Hunter finished.

"Yes, that's it," she said, "but Samantha would rather tag behind her big brothers. Poor thing, I know just how she feels."

"You have brothers?" he asked.

She pulled a notepad from the top drawer of her desk. "No. As a child, I dogged my father's footsteps. I wanted to go everywhere he went and do everything he did."

She stopped talking and rose from her chair. "How does an etiquette teacher forget to properly introduce herself?" She extended her hand. "I'm Ali Spencer."

"Hunter." He stood and briefly shook her outstretched hand, before they both took their seats.

"I understand this class was a gift, but it would

help if you told me a little about yourself, and why you're here?" She held a slim, pink pen poised in her hand for his reply.

Hunter took a deep breath and slowly released it. "I need you to turn me into Prince Charming, *for real.*"

Chapter Two

It figured. The first man to flip the switch on her long-forgotten libido was living in a fairy tale.

Ali dropped the pen and stared up at him. "Pardon me?"

He scrubbed a hand down his face and made a noise that came out as a half sigh, half groan. "My girlfriend says I'm rude."

"I see," Ali said, averting her gaze from his chiseled jaw, full lips, and intense brown eyes. Ordinary features, but on him they came together in a way that made her feel warm all over.

Ali had caught a glimpse of the woman who'd paid a bundle for his course when she'd come to the school a few days ago. Tall and reed thin, the supermodel look-alike had insisted on talking to the person in charge, so Aunt Rachel had dealt with her.

Now that Ali had seen Hunter Coleman, she couldn't help thinking what a striking couple he and the beautiful woman must make, turning heads in their wake.

Biting back a twinge of disappointment, she picked up the pen and jotted the word *girlfriend* on a blank page in her notebook.

His being taken was a good thing, she reminded herself. She didn't have time to obsess over him or any other man. She had things to do, namely get her aunt's school and then her own career back on track.

He fished a crumpled gift certificate from his pants' pocket and slid it across the desk.

"These classes were her gift to me." He said the word *gift* as if his girlfriend had presented him with a rabid skunk.

Typical, Ali thought. One thing their male clients had in common was etiquette school was never their idea. It usually came at the urging of a boss, public relations rep, or love interest. Even then, the man in question was a reluctant participant.

So her first rule was to get them comfortable with the notion, and second, show them there was more to etiquette than saying "thank you" and knowing which fork to use at a formal dinner.

"Detective Coleman—"

"Hunter," he corrected.

"Well, Hunter, I thought you might like to hear about some of the other gentlemen who've recently benefited from our classes."

"So I'm not the first to get roped into this?" A humorless chuckle accompanied his question.

Ali watched his eyes grow wide with interest as she rattled off the names of several prominent Tennessee Titans football players.

"Him? You're kidding me, right?"

Ali shook her head. "My aunt says he was one of her best students."

"But why?" Hunter asked, obviously trying to reconcile the image of one of the National Football League's most dominant linebackers with what he knew of etiquette classes.

"His job doesn't end when he leaves the field," she said. "His calendar is chock-full of charity fund-raisers and formal dinners."

Hunter nodded his understanding and seemed more receptive. So Ali went for the coup de grace. "We've even worked with Percy Tompkins Jr."

Hunter shrugged and shook his head, indicating he had no idea who she was talking about.

"Percy's better known as rapper Buck-tooth Killah."

Hunter's eyes widened. "That foulmouthed little punk was in charm school?"

"Percy was overwhelmed by his sudden fame and not handling media interviews or communicating with executives at his record label very well," Ali said. "So his handlers brought him to us, and he hasn't thrown a tantrum with reporters or his label since he completed the course," she said proudly.

Ali was relieved to notice Hunter had relaxed into his seat and was no longer eyeing the door.

"And like our other gentlemen, I'm sure you'll find a working knowledge of the rules of proper etiquette will have a positive impact on other areas of your life."

Hunter held up his hand, forestalling the remainder of her prepared spiel. "Look, I appreciate you trying to put me at ease, but save your breath."

He blew out a weary sigh. He looked like a man who had something to say, but wasn't quite sure how to put it.

"Here's the deal. Erica's recently come into money, and now she has her heart set on rubbing elbows with the city's elite. She envisions herself as an up-and-coming socialite-slash-philanthropist, and she believes I'm the reason those snobs haven't taken to her."

"Are you?" she asked, picking up on the note of disapproval in his tone. "Could it be you're unconsciously sabotaging her efforts?"

Hunter shrugged. "I'm not the kind of man who stands by and lets his date, or for that matter any woman, be insulted. It doesn't matter if we're having lobster at a fancy dinner or peanuts at a sports bar."

Ali didn't need details on the insults. She had a pretty good idea. After all, she'd come to Nashville after leaving one of south Florida's ritziest communities divorced, unemployed, and utterly humiliated.

"Erica's strategy has been to donate enormous

amounts of money to the pet causes of the chair-women of the so-called best boards and committees," Hunter continued. "While they have no problem accepting her checks, they don't seem any closer to inviting her to join their groups."

Ali started to tell him that Erica's approach was all wrong, but the pitying look on his face told her he already knew.

Ali found herself envying the woman, not for her wealth or having this hunky cop's heart, but because she had someone who cared enough to stand up for her. Not only had no one jumped to Ali's defense when she was being trashed, but the man who'd vowed to love her forever had been the one out to destroy her.

Ali forced back the ugly memories. Her focus should be on her client right now. His girlfriend was paying them a lot of money to get him country club ready, the funds they'd already put toward repairs on the school's dilapidated building.

She swallowed the lump of emotion lodged in her throat, before speaking. "I think our Manners Makeover for Gentlemen will smooth out some of your rough edges," Ali said.

She explained the details of the school's training for men, which would be handled by her aunt. "The flexible one-on-one coaching covers everything from greetings to table manners to socializing, especially with difficult people," she added pointedly.

"Your class sessions will be followed by real-life dress rehearsals," Ali said. "For example, after the formal dining lesson, you'll demonstrate your skills at a four-star restaurant."

"Well, I guess I'm in good hands," he finally said.

"Okay, let's get you signed up." She opened the folder on her desk and extracted a registration form. Once he filled it out, he'd be her aunt Rachel's problem.

He looked up from the form. "So, what's your success rate?" he asked, shifting in his seat. "Do you ever have students drop out or maybe even get kicked out?"

"You don't have to worry. My aunt Rachel will be your instructor, and in over forty years of teaching she's only had to expel two students," Ali said, "but that was years ago."

"Whoa!" He abandoned the form and raised his hands in a halting gesture. "I thought you would be my teacher."

Ali shook her head. "No, but I'm sure you'll be pleased with my aunt."

"I don't want her."

Ali cringed, taken aback by his blunt tone. "Excuse me?"

His dark brown eyes locked in on hers.

"I want you," he said slowly, making each word sound like a sentence on its own.

Goose bumps erupted on her arms, and she

couldn't stop the small gasp that escaped from between her lips.

"What I mean is I'd prefer a class you taught," he said hurriedly.

She swallowed hard, her mouth suddenly dry. "Sorry, but I'm only teaching youth classes right now."

When she joined the school, one of the first things she'd done was take over the children's classes. Aunt Rachel's stern, no-nonsense teaching style didn't go over well with today's kids.

Hunter shook his head. "I knew this was a dumb idea," he muttered under his breath. He rose from his chair. "Thanks for your time."

Panic mounted in Ali's chest as he strode toward the door. If she allowed him to leave like this, his girlfriend would demand a refund. Even worse, word could circulate around town that the school refused to accommodate him.

Ali couldn't chance either scenario.

"Wait! I'll be your instructor," she blurted out before she could think about it.

He stopped and slowly walked back to her desk. "Great," he said, visibly relieved. "How soon can we start? I want to get this over with."

Hmmph, Ali silently fumed. He wasn't the only one.

"So, you actually went through with it?"

"Yep." Hunter pulled his heel to his backside and held it until he felt the stretch in his quadriceps. He dropped his foot to the ground and repeated the prerun stretch on the other side.

Looking up, he caught his longtime friend and fellow detective's incredulous stare. "Close your mouth, Pete. It's not that big of a deal."

But Peter Jameson continued to gawk at him as if he'd turned down tickets to the Super Bowl to host a Tupperware party.

Hunter pushed off, beginning the pair's early morning run along the five-mile trail winding through the wooded park near Hunter's town house.

Pete fell into step beside him. "Damn, I thought for sure you'd punk out," he said. "Now I owe Bishop and Morrison twenty bucks."

"Don't tell me you told those two? They've got the biggest mouths in the precinct."

"It might have slipped out," Pete said with mild shame.

"Thanks a lot," Hunter said, wishing he hadn't confided in his friend. The other night, when he'd shown up at Pete and Sandy's house for poker without Erica, the whole story had tumbled out.

"Come on, man. You know I can hold my tongue. But charm school?" Pete sucked in a gulp of air as he pounded the paved trail. "What's next, ballet lessons?"

"First off, it's not charm school, it's a school of *etiquette*." Hunter emphasized the word as if putting some bass behind it would make it manlier.

"Whatever," Pete harrumphed.

"Secondly, I'll bet you didn't run your mouth to Sandy about it."

His friend nearly stumbled over his own feet, confirming Hunter's suspicion. At six foot four and over two hundred pounds, Pete's intimidating build and booming voice made him a cop most criminals didn't want to tangle with. But when it came to his wife and three young sons, the grizzly bear was more like a koala bear.

"Didn't think so," Hunter said, perversely grateful to see the smug smile wiped off Pete's face at the mention of Sandy's name. "Since you've made it common knowledge, I might as well clue her in."

"Don't!" Pete's tone held a touch of pleading.

They rounded a thicket of bushes signaling the half-mile mark, and Hunter kicked up the pace. "Last time I ate dinner at your place, didn't she mention how your barbaric table manners were rubbing off on your sons?"

"Come on, Hunt. You tell Sandy and she'll have me and my boys over at that school before you can say no elbows on the table," he said. "You wouldn't do that to your godsons, would you?"

"I don't know. Maybe it's just too good to keep to myself," he taunted.

"Okay, you made your point. I promise not to tell another soul."

Hunter nodded as he ducked to avoid a low-hanging tree branch. Lulled by the steady beat of his heart pumping and his sneakers slapping the ground, his mind drifted. He glanced over at a mother lifting her toddler up to the water fountain for a drink.

By now, he'd thought he and Erica would have been married and talking kids. At the rate they were going, he wondered if he ever would propose.

"So, what made you go through with it?" Pete broke the silence. "Last week you were fed up with her wannabe act, then yesterday you sign up for charm school."

How could he explain it to his friend, when he wasn't sure himself? All he knew was he was tired of coming home to his empty town house. At thirty-five, he was ready to give up his bachelorhood for the kind of family life Pete enjoyed. Yet after investing two years in his relationship with Erica, he wasn't eager to start over with someone new.

"The more I fight Erica on this socialite business, the more she digs in her heels," he said. "So I've decided to go along with it, until she can get it out of her system."

"How long do you think that will take?"

"I don't think it will be much longer. She's been at it for months and isn't any closer to getting in with them," he said. "Honestly, I doubt she ever will. She may have cash, but lacks an old-money pedigree."

"Then why bother with the manners brushup?"

"Erica and I had a good thing going before the money. Let's just say I owe her some effort and patience."

"Yeah, Erica used to be a great gal, but now . . ." Pete shook his head.

"What?"

"Nothing, man."

"You can tell me."

Pete heaved a sigh. "Sandy saw her yesterday at that fancy new restaurant downtown, when she was taking her mother out for a birthday lunch. She said she went over to Erica's table to say hello, and she acted like she barely knew her."

Hunter's mind flashed to Erica's comment about dumping deadweight, and he wondered if Sandy was one of her causalties. He opened his mouth to say something in her defense, but closed it. He couldn't defend the inexcusable.

"She and Sandy go back to nursing school. They've been friends a long time," Pete said.

Hunter swiped at the sweat rolling down his face with his forearm. "I don't like the way she's been acting either, but like I told you, I'm trying to be patient."

"I'm not sure her friends will be as understanding as you."

"It hasn't been easy," Hunter admitted.

"Erica's lucky. Another guy might only be with her for the money," Pete said. "I still can't believe you turned down the new Mercedes she'd bought for you."

"I don't want her money. If and when I get a Benz, I'll be the one buying it."

"But that was one sweet ride."

Hunter thought back to the sleek black luxury car he'd refused. "Working this job shows me enough of how low some people will sink to get their hands on things that don't belong to them."

"Amen."

"Speaking of work, anything new?"

"Got a call from Morrison. Two new residential break-ins, same as the rest."

Frustration washed over Hunter at more houses being robbed by a suspect or suspects they always seemed to be one step behind. "Damn, I'll be glad when we catch these ass—"

"Whoa!" Pete interrupted. "Now, that doesn't sound very charming. Looks like you may need to stay after class."

Images of Ali Spencer and her pink pelican-print dress floated through his mind. For some reason, staying after school didn't seem so bad.

Ali inhaled the curls of steam rising from the china teapot, hoping the fragrant scent of jasmine would put her aunt in a compromising mood.

"Do you have time for tea?" She stood at the threshold of the older woman's office holding a silver tray, already knowing the answer to the question. No matter the temperature, her Anglophile aunt never turned down hot tea.

Rachel Spencer Holmes looked up from the paperwork scattered across the antique desk that had once belonged to Ali's great-great-great-grandmother. She was dressed in a starched gray suit accessorized with pearls at her ears and around her slim neck. Despite the unseasonably warm spring weather and the building's lack of central air-conditioning, the older woman looked as she always did. Impeccable.

Her aunt's penetrating brown eyes darted from the tray to Ali's face and back again.

"Of course, dear."

Beckoning Ali inside, she tidied up the papers she'd been reviewing and tucked them into a drawer.

Ali set the tray on top of the weathered walnut desk. She bit the inside of her lip to keep from mentioning the untouched laptop at the opposite end. Using it would have helped her aunt accomplish the work more efficiently, but she'd stubbornly refused.

Baby steps, Ali reminded herself as she poured hot tea into the delicate, hand-painted cups. She moved a Queen Anne chair from across the room and seated herself on the other side of the desk. She'd drag this antiquated school and Aunt Rachel into the twenty-first century, she thought, sitting down, one baby step at a time.

"Oh my, another *colorful* ensemble." Her aunt squinted at Ali's pink seashell-print skirt and matching pink blouse. "I practically need sunglasses to look at you."

It wasn't the first time Aunt Rachel had pointed out her vibrant fashion choices. The bold colors of her Lilly Pulitzer–dominated wardrobe, which had flown under the radar in south Florida's lush tropical landscape, stood out like a pink elephant here in Nashville.

"I'm not buying new clothes, Auntie," Ali said, not that she could afford to these days anyway.

Fortunately, her aunt changed the subject.

"Impressive spread, Alison," she said, surveying the offerings on the desk. Pure delight brightened her sixty-nine-year-old, still-unlined face. "Jasmine tea, macaroons, strawberry scones, cream puffs. All of my favorites."

Her aunt bit into a cream puff and her eyes rolled heavenward. "Scrumptious," she said, and dabbed the corner of her mouth with a starched linen napkin from the tray.

"I remember you serving high tea every afternoon when Dad dumped me off on you for the summer."

"Don't be silly," her aunt said. "I loved having you. If John hadn't brought you, I would have come down to Florida and picked you up myself."

Ali sipped her tea. Back then, she hadn't wanted to leave her widowed father alone, but he'd insisted. After she'd lost her mother at four years old, he'd thought his tomboy of a daughter would benefit from his older sister's feminine influence.

Ali did. The summers she'd spent with her aunt and at the school eventually helped her snag a position at a major metropolitan newspaper after college. While the *South Florida Beacon* hadn't been interested in hiring a green reporter fresh out of journalism school, they'd had an opening for a Miss Manners–type to pen a weekly column.

Ali's take on infusing life's frantic pace with genteel elegance rapidly became a reader favorite, and her column was bumped up to twice weekly. Over the years, she parlayed the column's popularity into a series of books.

Her column was being considered for syndication, and she was in negotiations to host a local lifestyle television show, when everything went horribly wrong.

Now Ali was back where she started, at her aunt's school. Only now it was literally crumbling down around them.

Her aunt stirred a packet of sugar substitute into her tea, before taking a sip. The spoon clinked softly against the gold-rimmed cup, arousing Ali from her thoughts.

"I stopped by the hardware store to pick up a

few tools and materials. Now I can get started on some of these repairs," she said, figuring she'd start with an easy topic.

Her aunt nodded, but appeared more interested in selecting another treat.

"Oh, and I took your appointment with Mr. Coleman yesterday," Ali said.

"Thanks again for meeting with him. When Celia called to tell me she'd fallen, I had to go check on her," her aunt said. "So, how did it go?"

"He enrolled, but I'm going to be handling his instruction if you don't mind," Ali said, leaving out that he'd been adamant she do so.

"Are you sure? I was hoping for another crack at Hunter Coleman."

Ali put down her teacup. "You know him?"

"I haven't seen him since he was six, and I kicked both him and his brother out of my class. I called their mother and told her to come pick up those two hellions immediately."

"What did they do?"

Aunt Rachel shook her head. "Nearly tore the place apart, so they could get out of my class and go play baseball."

Ali helped herself to a scone. Now she understood why Hunter had insisted on her being his teacher instead of her aunt.

"Detective Coleman is only available evenings," Ali said. "It'll be easier if I just stay after the boys' class."

Aunt Rachel nodded her approval and then

focused her keen eyes on Ali. "So, what do you *really* want to talk to me about, dear?"

Ali exhaled, looking from the bakery-fresh treats to the older woman's stern face. So much for softening her up with sweets, she thought.

"I'd like you to reconsider the high-tech manners for children class," she said firmly.

She watched her aunt's lips tighten and wondered how she managed to get her next sip of tea past them.

"High tech and manners are an oxymoron," Aunt Rachel finally said. Her dulcet tone, sweeter than any cream puff, disguised her bullheadedness. "There's no such thing."

"That's exactly why we should offer this class. How can we expect kids to grow into adults who turn off their cell phones at restaurants or don't stop midconversation to check their e-mail if they don't know any better?"

"Cell phones, PDAs, MP3s, and the rest of those techno gadgets are just noisy nuisances."

"Maybe, but they're here to stay," Ali said. "The school has to change with the times."

The corners of her aunt's mouth turned down in a full-fledged frown. "Four generations of Spencer women have run this school for over a hundred years. They steered it through two world wars, Jim Crow, the Depression, and the civil rights movement."

Instinctively, Ali looked up at the portraits lining the wall behind her aunt. They ranged from brown-tinged sepia and black-and-white likenesses of the grandmothers she'd never known to the color likeness of her aunt.

"Soon it will be your turn. Then you can do what you want. Until then—"

Ali cut her off. "Auntie, you know I'm only here temporarily. Once I get the school profitable and this old building back in shape, I'm leaving."

"For where? Did you get a job offer you haven't told me about?"

"No, but you need to get the idea of me staying here and taking over the school out of your mind."

"Fine." Her aunt sniffed. "So stop trying to change everything. I refuse to relax the Spencer standards."

Ali bit into a scone to take the edge off her frustration, but it failed to soothe her. She hadn't thought much about the school until her aunt's call four months ago.

The request for help had come at a time when Ali had needed something to focus on besides the humiliation of her failed marriage and career. Nashville had sounded like as good a place as any to lick her wounds and plot her comeback.

Before she'd return to her real life, she was determined to make her family's history-steeped etiquette school relevant and profitable in today's world. If her aunt would only cooperate.

"I admit, I've made a lot of changes since I've arrived," Ali said finally, "but I don't believe any of them compromise our standards."

Her aunt shook her head. "It's too much change. Too fast. I think we should wait out all this high-tech nonsense," she countered. "Good manners never go out of style."

"You have to admit the princess tea parties and after-school program piqued more interest in the school. Both are nearly half-full." Ali defended the two classes she'd recently added.

"Hmmph," her aunt snorted. "With all the giggles and laughter, it sounds like they're doing more playing than learning."

Ali didn't take the bait. She wouldn't allow herself to be pulled into another debate on teaching styles.

"So, do I have your permission to give the Techno Manners class a try?"

Her aunt waved a dismissive hand. "I'll think about it."

It was a gesture that usually silenced Ali, but not this time. She thought about the school's growing stack of bills and the repairs that needed doing around the older building, and she continued to push.

"It's time to stop sitting on the sidelines waiting for things to return to the way we want them to be and do something." Otherwise there wouldn't be any Spencer school, she thought.

Her aunt put the macaroon she'd raised to her lips back on the plate, and raised her eyes to meet Ali's gaze. "Isn't that exactly what I've been telling you for weeks?"

Here we go, Ali thought.

"We're not talking about me," Ali replied. She knew where her aunt was steering this conversation and she didn't like it.

"Have you given *my* suggestion any consideration since *you* promised to *think it over*?" her aunt asked, oblivious of Ali's protest.

"I'm not ready to date. It's too soon."

Her aunt sipped her tea. "Don't be ridiculous. You're a divorcée, not a widow. Besides, your divorce has been final for almost a year."

"I appreciate your concern, but there isn't a man alive I'd be interested in going out with." Ali braced herself for the wave of bitterness usually accompanying the statement, but it didn't come. Instead, her mind conjured up images of Hunter Coleman.

She closed her eyes briefly to banish her handsome new student from her thoughts and focused on bringing up an image of his girlfriend instead.

"Did you hear what I said, dear?"

"Sorry, no." Ali straightened in her chair.

"I was telling you about Celia's nephew, Edward. You remember Celia?" the older woman continued, not waiting for an answer. "He's divorced too, and Celia thinks you two would hit it off. Then there's also a nice single man from church—"

"Thanks, Aunt Rachel, but no," Ali said firmly, hoping to stop her matchmaking before it got started.

"Well, you don't have to get so snippy about it." Her aunt sniffed. "You want me to be open to your suggestions, but you refuse to extend me the same courtesy."

"That's unfair. I'm talking business, and you're trying to interfere in my personal life."

"What personal life?" her aunt asked. "You spend all of your time here."

"So do you," Ali countered.

"That's why I'm pushing you so hard to get back into the dating world, so you don't end up like me. Looking back, I wish I'd listened to friends who'd encouraged me to date again after your uncle died," she said. "It's hard growing old alone."

Ali averted her eyes from the regret lurking in her aunt's gaze.

"No," she said.

"One date, Alison. Just one little date."

"No."

"How about if I agree to let you start your high-tech etiquette class? On a trial basis, of course."

Ali dropped the smooth manners her aunt had drummed into her since childhood. "Let me get this straight." She leaned forward in her chair. "The only way I get the class is if I let you pimp me out?"

Her aunt's lips curved into a sweet smile. "I don't consider asking you to go on an innocent blind date 'pimping,' but yes, that's the gist of it."

Ali exhaled a long, exasperated breath. "Fine, I'll do it."

"That's wonderful, dear." Her aunt clasped her hands together. "You won't regret it. When you meet Edward, you'll be thanking your old aunt."

Ali groaned inwardly. Somehow she doubted it.

Chapter Three

Ali spread the damask linen tablecloth over the rickety table.

It still wobbled a bit, despite the book she'd wedged underneath the leg. But like everything else around the ancient school, it would have to do.

Fortunately, she'd brought the bulk of her table accoutrements with her to Nashville. The last time she'd used them had been for a dinner party she and Brian had hosted with a guest list that included Florida's lieutenant governor and several important local dignitaries. Now the platinum-rimmed ivory plates would simply create a good representation of the formal table settings Hunter Coleman would likely encounter when he was out with his rich girlfriend.

His girlfriend.

Ali would do good to remember the fact.

Not that his relationship status mattered. Her

own life was in such disarray, the last thing she needed in it was a man.

Pulling back the cardboard flaps on the carton containing her wedding china, Ali remembered the concerned look on Aunt Rachel's face when she'd brought it to the school. Her aunt had asked several times if she was sure she wanted to use the expensive, once-special plates.

She plunked the elegant soup bowls, then salad plates down on the table. She didn't care if they were accidently chipped, cracked, or even smashed to bits.

Ali was certain all right. Like her marriage, they no longer held any sentimental value.

Ali paused, her ears perking up.

There it goes again, she thought.

The nearly constant sound of trickling water coming from the bathroom down the hall pricked her nerves as she arranged the plates, then added flatware and glasses.

She'd already picked up the repair supplies, and her tools were in her office. Hopefully she could put a stop to that running toilet before Hunter arrived.

She glanced at her wristwatch. He'd be here in less than an hour. She fussed with a fork, even though they wouldn't be eating.

Finally, she took a step back and admired the beautifully set table. If it were anywhere but here, one would think it was a romantic table for two at a four-star restaurant.

However, this beautifully set formal table was all business—exactly as Ali would be when she saw Hunter Coleman.

Hunter listened to Erica's recorded voice instructing the caller to leave a message.

Not bothering to leave another one, he flipped his cell phone closed and returned it to the holder clipped to his belt. So much for Erica giving him a reason not to scrap this charm school crap and join the other detectives on his shift, who were by now on their second round of beers.

Heaving a weary sigh, he shut off the basketball game on the radio and threw open the driver's-side door of his black Dodge Challenger. During work hours he drove a department-issued Chevy Malibu, but on his own time he preferred his own ride.

Hunter had given Erica his word. That alone would have to be reason enough not to blow off his first etiquette class.

He used the short walk from the curb to the school's door to push images of watching tonight's basketball playoff game on a sixty-three-inch flat-screen at Big Johnny's sports bar from his mind.

He was here now. He yanked open the front door. Might as well make the best of it.

There was no one in the reception area, but the lights were still on, so he figured someone had to be around.

"Hello," he called out.

"I'm in here," Ali said.

Hunter wasn't sure exactly where "in here" was, but he followed her voice down the hallway to the ladies' room door.

"You okay in there?" he asked, through the slightly cracked door, wondering if she had taken ill.

"Sure, come on in."

The splintered door squeaked against its rusty hinges as he slowly pushed it open. Hunter wasn't sure what he'd expected to find. Twelve years of serving and protecting the public had taught him to anticipate anything.

Still, the last thing he expected to see was Ali, in a pink palm-tree-print dress, pearls around her neck and her arms buried up to the elbows in a toilet tank.

"What's wrong with it?" he asked, wondering if it was something he could fix. Hell, if he had a choice between a charm school lesson and rescuing her from a broken toilet, he'd take the toilet.

"It's been running," she said. "So I'm replacing the flapper."

From its subway-station-green walls to the tiny black-and-white hexagonal floor tiles, the bathroom was a throwback to another era. It was as if time had marched ahead and left it back in the 1950s.

"Want me to take a look at it for you?"

"No, thank you, I'm almost done," she said, not bothering to look up from the tank.

He watched her crouch down and turn on the water at the shut-off valve. When the tank filled, she flushed it and waited a few moments.

"Great, it drained. No need to adjust the chain or trip lever," she said more to herself than him.

She exhaled before looking at him. "We've got a lot of ground to cover this evening. Give me a second to wash up, and I'll be right with you," she said. "Everything is already set up in the classroom down the hall and on the right. It's two doors down from my office. You remember where my office is, don't you?"

Hunter scratched his head as he retreated, his brain struggling to reconcile the image of the petite, pink-clad manners expert with the apparently capable, amateur plumber.

His initial dread returned full force as he walked into the classroom. Front and center was a table set for two and loaded with enough perfectly arranged crystal, china, and cutlery to serve a dozen people.

Ali joined him a few moments later.

"Looks like I owe you another apology. Sorry to have kept you waiting again. I meant to have that project done before you arrived, but it took longer than I'd expected."

"I admit, I didn't expect to find you up to your elbows in a toilet," he chuckled.

She shrugged. "It's an old building. Unfortunately, my list of repairs is longer than my arm."

"So you're the handyman . . . eh, I mean handywoman . . . as well as teacher here."

Ali nodded.

"I'm impressed."

She smiled at him. Not the perfunctory smile he'd seen her give to the little girls' mothers the other day or the cool one she'd used with him. This genuine smile reached her eyes and warmed her entire face.

"My aunt taught me formal dinner protocol, but it was my dad who made sure I knew how to handle a toolbox," she said. "He's a plumber by trade, but there isn't anything he can't fix."

"Really? I'm in the process of rehabbing a 1920s bungalow," Hunter blurted out before he realized it, and for the life of him, he didn't know why he said it to her, of all people.

He rarely talked about the house left to him by his grandmother. He hadn't mentioned it to Erica or told his family he'd gone back inside the house after all these years, let alone let them know he'd started renovations.

"Sounds like a big job."

"I'd thought so, but the structure is sound. It just needs some elbow grease." He thought of the tiny dent he'd made in the long to-do list. "Lots of it."

"I'd love to see it sometime." Her small hand went to her mouth, and he was disappointed to see her high-wattage smile dim. She looked as if she wanted to take back her words.

"That would be great," he said, wondering what he'd said to spook her. "I just finished the kitchen, and I haven't had a chance to show it off yet."

The generic version of her smile returned as she nodded, and he could practically feel the wall go up around her. He didn't know Ali Spencer, but whoever had hurt her had done a helluva job.

"We're going to cover formal dining tonight," she said, directing his attention to the table.

"That's a lot of forks," he said. And glasses and plates, he thought.

Sure, he'd attended the occasional formal event for work and managed to eat without making an ass of himself. Then again, he suspected his fellow diners hadn't known any more about the correct fork to use than he had.

"It's not as complicated as it looks," Ali said.

Yeah, right, he thought, figuring the line was an etiquette teacher's version of the dentist's "this won't hurt a bit."

"Seriously, it's really simple," she said. "I tend to start with formal dining because it's the easiest lesson."

"If you say so," he said, unconvinced.

"First, I like to get my basic dinner no-nos

out of the way. Some of them may seem obvious to you, but I always like to make sure my clients and I are on the same page."

"Okay, shoot."

"No smacking, finger licking, teeth sucking, burping, cell phones"—she paused to breathe—"and absolutely no dangling a toothpick from your lips."

"You actually have to tell people this?"

Ali rolled her eyes skyward. "You'd be surprised," she said. "But if you already know better and are a quick study, I just might be able to get you out of here in time to catch the second half of the basketball game."

"How'd you know?" he asked, surprised.

She glanced at the small *Memphis Grizzlies* emblem on his polo shirt. "I figured you for a fan," she said.

Hunter felt his facial muscles twitch upward into the beginnings of smile, and he rubbed his hands together. "Well, what are we waiting on? Let's get to it."

She sidled up next to him, and he caught the scent of her perfume. The fragrance was the same fresh, citrusy scent.

"First, you need to make sure you're reaching for your own bread plate and water glass." Ali pointed to a small plate, the entrée plate and a glass. "Your bread plate will always be on your left and your water glass to your right. An easy way to remember this are the letters *B M W*, like the car, but in this case it stands for bread, meal, and water."

"Got it," he said. The quicker he caught on, the sooner he could get out of here.

"Okay, then have a seat and we'll move on to silverware."

Ali spent the next hour briefing him on the fine points of formal dining. He had to admit she was right. It wasn't nearly as complicated as the arsenal of tableware suggested.

"Now we'll go over it one last time, only you'll point out the utensils and their purpose to me."

She reached over to put a fish fork back into place at the same time he went for his salad fork. Their hands brushed, and she drew back as if she'd been burned.

"Is something wrong?"

She shook her head. "No," she said, averting her eyes. "I'm just waiting on you to get started so we can wrap up for the evening."

Hunter recapped the lesson, even remembering to leave his knife and fork in the position she said would signal a waiter he was done.

"Excellent," she said.

He wasn't sure why, but Ali's praise made him feel good. "Is that it?"

She nodded. "Next lesson, we're going to put what you learned tonight in action with real food in a formal atmosphere. Instead of here, we'll meet at the restaurant," she said, then filled him in on the time and place.

All through the lesson he'd only looked forward to the end of it. Now that it was over, he wasn't so eager to leave. Ali Spencer had piqued his curiosity.

Hunter knew she was none of his business, but his teacher intrigued him. He looked forward to finding out more about this enigma of a woman at the next lesson, over dinner.

How on earth was she going to get through another lesson with him?

Ali peeled the silver foil off another chocolate and dropped the wrapper atop the growing pile accumulating on her kitchen countertop.

Popping the candy into her mouth, she recalled how an accidental brush of his hand had nearly made her jump out of her skin. However, the sweet, creamy chocolate failed to erase the memory of contact so electric she'd wondered if he'd felt it too.

"Get it together," she scolded herself.

Catching the blinking red light on her answering machine out the corner of her eye, Ali jabbed the button and then crossed her fingers.

Hopefully, her agent, Leo, was finally returning her calls and had good news. Or maybe one of the résumés she'd sent out had caught a newspaper's interest.

Leo's voice filled the one-bedroom garden apartment, and for a nanosecond, she allowed herself to feel a sliver of optimism.

"Just getting back with you," he said. "Again, nothing's changed, but I'll give you a call if something breaks."

She grabbed another piece of candy from the open bag on the counter. Why did she even bother? Nobody was looking to hire a disgraced etiquette expert. Not after the smear job her ex-husband and her former best friend had done on her.

A digitized voice announced the time of the second message.

"Hi, Alison. It's Edward Wilson. Our aunts are friends. Anyway, I thought you might like to go out sometime. Give me a call."

Ali gave the machine an eye roll and scribbled his number on the pad she kept by the phone. Edward sounded like a nice enough guy, but she wasn't interested. She'd go out with him, but only on one date and only to get her aunt off her back.

The third message was from her friend and a sports columnist for her former paper, Lynn. Ali pressed FAST FORWARD to the forth, then fifth message both from Lynn. Then the phone rang, in the middle of Lynn's third message, startling Ali.

It was Lynn. Again.

Ali snatched up the receiver. "What on earth is it?"

"I'm been trying to reach you all evening. How come you aren't answering your cell?"

"Late class." Toeing off her shoes, Ali padded over to the living room with the bag of candy and sat down on the sofa. She eased back onto the cushions. "So, what's going on?"

"I wanted to tell you before word got out," Lynn started. "I know you were hoping the paper would reconsider and ask you to come back, after the whole hubbub settled down, but . . ."

Ali's stomach did a free fall to her toes. "They found a replacement, didn't they?"

"They hired Kay."

Ali stood abruptly, sending chocolates flying across the nondescript beige carpeting. Not her, she thought fiercely.

First, Brian. Now her job.

"Al, are you there?"

"Yes, I'm here," Ali croaked.

"I'm sorry, Al. I didn't want to tell you, but I'd hate to see you blindsided by the news."

"But I don't understand," Ali stammered. "How can they take her seriously as a journalist or an expert on protocol? She was an unemployed Web designer when I hired her to be my assistant."

"I know. I asked the same thing when I marched into the powers-that-be offices the moment I heard. They claim the combination of what she learned from you and her Web background will help them branch out beyond print and attract more online readers."

"Oh," Ali said softy, still absorbing the fact that

she'd trained the woman, who'd stolen her husband, to take her job.

"I know you're too polite to say it, but it's a load of crap and we both know it. They do too."

Although, after the paper had let her go they'd implied she could eventually be rehired, she'd known it was a long shot. Still, deep down she'd held out hope.

This sealed it.

No column. No new book deal. No television show. Her life as south Florida's guru on proper behavior really was over.

"Thanks for telling me, Lynn."

"Come on, girl. You're in a new city making a fresh start," her friend said.

Fresh start? She was treading water at a school that would close soon if she couldn't generate more business. Ali beat back a wave of self-pity as she hung up the phone.

For a fresh start, this felt an awful lot like rock bottom.

Chapter Four

Erica Boyd paced the length of her living room, the plush velvet carpet absorbing her angry steps.

She didn't like what she was hearing.

The fact that she was paying a lot of money for poor results irked her even more.

"I'm so sorry, Miss Boyd," her latest publicist said.

Erica stopped midstep and glared at her, somewhat gratified to see the dark circles under her eyes. She had summoned the woman to her penthouse at dawn, moments after the morning paper had arrived, and she'd seen the glaring omission.

Carrie McDaniel had showed within the hour, balancing a box of warm Krispy Kreme donuts and two vanilla lattes, which Erica assumed she'd brought to mollify her.

The publicist sat on a gold-cushioned armchair, while Erica stomped back and forth in front of her, still dressed in her ivory, silk dressing gown. Carrie wore a bland beige pantsuit.

Her hair, usually flat-ironed straight, was a halo of springy red curls surrounding her freckled face, and her bleary eyes were glued to the open society page on her lap.

Erica snatched the paper. She stared at the photos from the art exhibition again. Maybe if she stared at them long enough, her likeness would magically appear.

"I sponsored this stupid artist and his stupid showing," she ranted, thumping the paper with her hand. "Yet I'm not in any of these pictures. They didn't even mention my name!"

"I don't know how this happened," Carrie said.

"It's your job to ensure that something like this doesn't happen." Erica tossed the newspaper onto an end table and it landed with a thump next to Carrie's fat-laden offerings. She'd already fired two publicists and another had quit on her.

But she'd had high hopes for Carrie. The young woman had just opened up her own firm and was eager to please. She'd also come up with the brilliant suggestion to smooth down Hunter's rough edges with a bit of charm school.

Hunter.

The memory of him in her bed sent a delicious shiver from Erica's core down to her slipper-shod toes. Unfortunately, outside the bedroom their relationship was sliding rapidly downhill.

She loved the envious looks she got from

other women when she stepped into a room on Hunter's arm. She didn't want to let him go, unless she absolutely had to. She hoped she could count on that prissy old bat at the Spencer School to do her job and get him in line.

However, if Carrie didn't do a better job of garnering her some good publicity, she wouldn't hesitate to let her go.

"Did you position yourself close to the artist when the photographers were around, like we talked about?" Carrie asked.

"Of course I did." Erica snatched the paper off the table and pointed out a photo of the artist standing next to a couple, who'd raved over his watercolor rendition of a moonlit forest.

Erica had thought a toddler with a box of crayons could have produced a better "masterpiece," but had fallen into line with the majority and feigned delight over his use of light and angles.

"There's my arm. I recognize my diamond and sapphire bracelet and my cocktail ring," she said. "As you can see, the rest of me was cropped out."

"But I talked to the reporter personally," Carrie said.

Erica shook her head. "Your job is to get me press and attention, and I'm not happy with your lack of results."

"Please, Miss Boyd." Carrie stood. "We've only

just started working together. I assure you I'm up for the job. Please, give me a chance to prove myself."

Erica sighed. "Okay, you want to prove you're worth all the money I'm paying you?"

"I assure you, I am." Carrie nodded.

Erica flipped the paper over and pointed to an item she'd circled in red. "The Library Ball is coming up."

Carrie nodded. "It's the most exclusive party in town this month."

"I know, and I haven't received an invitation yet," Erica said pointedly. "I want you to make sure I do."

Carrie gulped audibly. "I'll check into the oversight."

"And, Carrie, while you're here there's something else I want to talk to you about." She gestured for the publicist to retake her seat, and she sat down on the sofa adjacent to it.

Erica pulled an old copy of *Music City* magazine off the coffee table. NASHVILLE'S MOST BEAU-TIFUL SOCIALITES, the headline boasted. "I want to be on the cover of this magazine."

Ali backed her Honda into a free space near the coffeehouse where she'd agreed to meet Edward for their blind date. She'd been relieved when he'd suggested having a casual cup of coffee rather than a full-blown meal.

It would make the blind date ordeal less torturous.

"You're here now, so you might as well make the best of it," she muttered as she walked through the open door.

Upbeat jazz and the aroma of fresh-ground coffee greeted her on the inside of the place, which by the looks of the crowd was a hangout for college students and twenty-somethings.

Her eyes scanned the occupied bistro tables and overstuffed chairs for a man clad in the khaki pants and black shirt Edward said he'd be wearing. The problem was she'd already spotted three men sporting the combination.

"Alison?"

Hearing her name, Ali turned in the direction of the voice and her jaw dropped to her chest. "Edward?"

He nodded. "I hope you haven't been waiting long."

Her gaze flickered over his T-shirt. It was black, all right, but emblazoned with the likeness of her former client Percy Tompkins in his Buck-tooth Killah persona, and the khakis turned out to be khaki cargo pants that rode way too low on Edward's behind.

Yet, it wasn't his wardrobe choices that had Ali's mouth gaped open like a beached fish struggling for air. Celia's *nephew* had to be at least seventy years old.

"It's Ali," she stammered, "and I just got here myself."

He winked, deepening the crinkles around his eye. "Good. I'd hate to start off on the wrong foot by being rude to an etiquette teacher."

Ali spied another look at him. His head was shaved bald and oversized diamond studs sparkled from his earlobes, in what she guessed was an attempt to look younger. However, his efforts were neutralized by the steel gray of his mustache and bushy eyebrows.

"Looks like there's a free table over there." Edward gestured to the right side of the room. "If you'll grab it, I'll get our coffees."

Ali gave him her drink order and made her way over to the table. She was going to strangle her aunt when she saw her. She also planned to get a lot more out of her than permission to start a high-tech manners class.

Aunt Rachel owed her big time.

Moments later, Edward arrived at the table with two of the largest cups of coffee she'd ever seen.

"Wow!" Ali commented on the size of the coffees as he sat down.

He flashed her a proud smile and a dimple-turned-wrinkle creased his cheek. "With my senior discount, I can get a large cup for the same price as the small."

"Soooo, you're Celia's *nephew?*" His voice had sounded much younger on the phone.

He chuckled before taking a sip of coffee. "I can see where you might be confused. Aunt Celia was an unexpected midlife surprise for my grandparents. My grandma was twenty when she had my mother and forty-nine when Celia came along."

Realization dawned on Ali as he explained the family connection. "Oh, I get it now," she said. And her own dear aunt was going to get an earful.

"I can still remember when my grandparents brought her home from the hospital," Edward said. "I was around five or so."

Ali took an unladylike gulp of her coffee, not sure of what else to say to her *date*.

"Celia mentioned you went through a rough divorce," he said.

Ali nodded. "I survived," she said. "What about you? You're divorced too, right?"

"Yep, after nearly forty years of marriage."

"How sad. What happened?"

Although she knew it was in poor taste to ask someone she'd just met something so personal, she couldn't help herself. After four decades, it seemed like such a shame for a marriage to have ended in divorce.

Ali heard a buzzing sound. Edward looked down at the flashing cell phone clipped to his belt, and he began fishing around in a low side pocket of his cargo pants. He retrieved a Bluetooth earpiece and stuck it in on his ear.

"Hello," he shouted into the earpiece loud enough for half the coffeehouse to hear. Some people turned around, but after seeing it was just an old guy who looked like he was adjusting the volume on his hearing aid, they turned back to their own conversations.

"No, I can't hang out with you guys today." His stuck his finger in his other ear and his voice grew louder. "I'm on a date."

His last line garnered them a giggle from a college-aged girl at the next table, while her companion gave Edward a thumbs-up sign. "Handle your business, gramps," he said.

Ali took another gulp of coffee, wishing she could dive into the enormous cup and hide.

Edward finished his call and turned his attention back to her. "Now where were we?"

"You were telling me—"

"Oh, now I remember," he interrupted. "We were talking about my divorce."

Ali shook her head to forestall him. "Really, I shouldn't have asked. It's none of my business."

"My wife acted like an old fart," Edward said. "All she ever wanted to do was hang out at the senior citizen center or babysit our great-grandchildren. Don't get me wrong, I love those kids. But I didn't want to spend the rest of my life babysitting and hanging out with a bunch of old people."

He leaned forward and folded his arms on

the table. Ali noted the light dusting of silver hairs on his forearms and the liver spots on his brown hands.

"I know this probably isn't the politically correct thing to say, but old folks just ain't my bag," he said.

It was all Ali could do not to dig her compact out of her purse and hold up the mirror for him to take a good look at himself.

She'd upheld her side of the deal she'd made with Aunt Rachel. Now it was time for her to cut this date short. She glanced at her watch. "Where does the time go? I have a ton of stuff to do today."

"But you haven't finished your coffee."

"Oh, I couldn't possibly drink all this coffee."

A slow grin spread across Edward's face. "How about we finish drinking them at my place? My Escalade is parked outside."

"Thanks, but no, thanks," Ali said, not feeling quite so polite. She picked her purse up off the floor.

"Wait!" Edward pulled a prescription bottle from his pocket and slid it toward the center of the table.

Ali looked down at the bottle. "Are those your heart pills? Do you need me to get you a glass of water?" she asked, concerned.

Edward laughed. "I know what you're thinking. You figure I'm too old." He picked up the bottle of pills and shook it. "But these magic pills have changed the game. I pop two of these babies, and I can put it on you for hours."

Ali stared at him a moment as his meaning sank in, and then she jumped from her chair so fast it fell backward to the floor.

"I can go like a jackhammer," Ali heard him call out to her as she bolted out the door.

For the first time since her divorce, Ali felt lucky. Edward's poor wife had spent forty years with a man who turned out to be a jackass.

Thanks to her former best friend, Ali had found out her ex-husband was one early on, and now she had her entire life ahead of her.

Chapter Five

Hunter's stomach growled, reminding him he hadn't eaten since lunch the day before. Not that he needed reminding. Hunger pangs had struck around ten that morning and continued to plague him throughout his busy workday.

He'd skipped dinner last night to finish scraping off old wallpaper at the house he'd inherited from his grandmother, and then missed both breakfast and lunch today chasing leads on a growing stack of unsolved burglaries.

Now he was starved out of his mind.

Hunter followed the hostess as she weaved through the dining room of the upscale restaurant Ali had selected for the follow-up to his formal dining lesson. He stuck a finger down the collar of the dress shirt he'd hurriedly changed into to loosen the chokehold of his silk tie.

Muted colors, soft music, and candlelight marked the tasteful décor, but Hunter barely noticed the atmosphere. All he cared about was how fast they could get hot food in front of him and then keep it coming.

He spotted Ali as they approached the table. Instead of her usual ponytail, her hair fell around her shoulders in soft, tousled waves. She should wear it down more often, he thought. It looked good.

"Hope I didn't keep you waiting long." He seated himself across from her.

Her brown eyes widened and she smiled approvingly. "You look handsome."

Hunter smoothed his tie. He'd brought the navy suit to work with him this morning and changed into it after his shift had ended. He'd ignored Pete, who along with Bishop and Morrison couldn't resist teasing him.

"Well, if it's not Cinderfella," Morrison had said, causing Bishop to bend over with laughter. "Will you turn into a pumpkin at midnight?"

Hunter had looked over at the two of them and shaken his head. "Maybe if you two put on some decent clothes once in a while, you'd be having dinner with a woman tonight, instead of each other."

"Don't look at me, I have a wife," Pete had said before launching into a description of the dinner his wife, Sandy, had waiting on him.

Their joking, although good-natured, had annoyed Hunter.

However, Ali's comment had the opposite effect and he was glad he'd made the effort.

"I believe we can skip the appearance lesson," she said. "You obviously don't need it."

The hunger pangs started up again and he reached for his menu. Reading the descriptions of food, any food, only made his empty belly cramp in protest, so he snapped it shut.

"I heard the salmon is excellent here," Ali offered.

Hunter nodded politely, knowing there was no way fish would appease his appetite. "I'll go with the steak."

After what seemed like hours, but was in reality only a few minutes, their tuxedo-clad waiter arrived. Only he wasn't the waiter.

"Sir, I'm the wine steward," he said. "Your waiter will be with you shortly."

Hunter glanced over at Ali. He did remember her explaining some formal restaurants had wine stewards or sommeliers to help with wine selection.

Meanwhile, the guy talked on and on about red, white, dry, the perfect complement to fish, poultry, meat, but his words sounded like *blah, blah, blah* to Hunter's ears.

Hunter looked enviously at diners near their table and wished he were eating. Couldn't they at least bring out some bread? Especially if this guy was going to yap about wine half the evening, he thought.

He took a deep breath and willed himself to be cool. After all, the man was just doing his job.

By the time the waiter showed up, Hunter's hunger pangs had migrated to his head and into a dreaded, hungry headache. His fingertips drummed on the tabletop as he waited for Ali to make her selections.

"Is everything okay?" She paused, her eyes zeroing in on his impatient fingers.

Realizing what he was doing, Hunter halted the impromptu percussion solo. "Sorry," he muttered.

When it was his turn, he quickly rattled off his order. He resisted the temptation to offer the guy a hundred bucks to get his dinner on the table in under a minute.

"So tell me about yourself?" he asked Ali, hoping conversation would take his mind off food as well as satisfy his curiosity.

She shrugged, and for the first time he noticed how her sleeveless black dress accentuated her shapely arms.

"There isn't much to tell," she said. "I've only been in town a few months."

He took a sip of water, preferring not to drink wine on an empty stomach. "So, what brought you from Florida to Nashville?"

"How did you know I was from Florida?" She stiffened.

"I read it on the back of your book when I was in your office the other day."

A bit relieved, she answered, "I'm here to help my aunt out at the school."

It didn't take a detective to figure out there was more to the story. Why would an author and big-city newspaper columnist want to teach in an old school that was practically falling apart?

Hunter had started to ask her another question when the sight of their waiter bearing soup and bread caught his attention. Thank God, he thought. He could practically feel his belly button sinking into his spine.

The waiter set the bread in front of him, and Hunter's appetite overwhelmed any thoughts of manners. It was as if a checkered flag had been waved in front of his stomach, signaling it to *go*.

Reaching past the watery bowl of soup, Hunter snatched a roll from the basket. He ripped it apart with his hands and shoved half of it into his mouth.

Then he caught Ali's narrowed gaze.

He opened his mouth, intending to explain he hadn't eaten all day, but his hand stuffed the other half of the roll into it.

Her eyes widened.

Okay, one more, he thought, and then he'd simply tell her he was hungry, *really hungry*. Only by the time he'd eaten another roll and then another, their entrées had arrived.

He looked down at the miniscule steak. His plate looked as if someone had spent hours painstakingly decorating it with various sauces. The side vegetables were also artfully arranged.

It wasn't much, especially considering his

mammoth appetite, but he grabbed the closest knife and fork and dug in. Two minutes later, he was done and wondering how many of these plates he'd have to order to make a real meal.

He peered over at Ali, who had barely touched her fish. Her gaze flickered to his empty plate before coming to rest on his face.

"Well, now that you've flunked formal dining . . ." She took a sip of wine. "Shall we order dessert?"

Ali wasn't surprised when the answer to her question was yet another violent growl coming from the direction of Hunter's stomach.

"This is some kind of reality show stunt, right?" She glanced around the restaurant. "Those growling noises are coming from a speaker under the table, and any minute the waiter is going to come back with Ashton Kutcher in tow and tell me I've been *Punk'd*."

She took another sip of her wine as she waited for him to expose the cameramen and let her in on the joke. It might have sounded far-fetched, but it was the only explanation she could think of for the way he'd practically attacked every morsel of food put in front of him.

"Nothing that sinister," Hunter said. "Work has been crazy lately, and I haven't had a bite since yesterday afternoon."

"You should have said something," she exclaimed. "We could have rescheduled."

Hunter shrugged. "I figured since our lesson was in a restaurant, we could kill two birds so to speak."

She heard his stomach growl again. "You can have mine."

She looked at her plate as she slid it toward him. The cut of salmon was tiny.

Her aunt had raved about the service at this restaurant, but had cautioned the portions ran small. Still, she liked to use it for training because they set a wonderful formal table.

Hunter shook his head. "No, thanks. I'll pass on dessert too, which I'm guessing will be the size of a breath mint."

He leaned forward and crossed his arms on the table. "I was thinking along the lines of some real food. You know, slow-cooked pot roast, smothered in its own gravy and topped with sliced red potatoes, baby carrots, pearl onions, and celery."

Ali licked her lips as he continued.

"A slab of homemade bread on the side and a big hunk of black forest cake for dessert."

The next growl she heard might have come from her own stomach. She was too entranced by the images he'd conjured up in her head to know for sure.

Not having the energy or the inclination to bother cooking a meal for just one person, she'd existed on frozen diet dinners since she'd arrived in Nashville four months ago. The nuked meals had been hot and fast, and that had been good enough—until now.

Ali could practically smell the mouthwatering aroma of Hunter's fantasy meal, and her deprived taste buds danced in anticipation.

"Sounds delicious. Unfortunately, they don't serve that here," she said.

A mischievous spark lit up his dark brown eyes. "I know where they do," he said. "Care to join me?"

Ali shook her head no, just as her common sense directed. But her mouth refused to follow suit.

"I'd love to," she heard herself say aloud, then tried to backpedal. "I mean . . . I'd love to any other time, but I can't," she stammered.

Hunter's brow creased. "Why not?"

Ali shifted in her seat, the high-back chair suddenly becoming uncomfortable. *Because I'm attracted to you.*

"Don't tell me I'm the only one still hungry. You were practically slobbering when I described that melt-in-your-mouth meal."

"Slobbering? I don't slobber," she said, feeling a smile tug at the corners of her mouth.

He reached for his wallet and signaled for the waiter. "Let's get out of here."

"The meal's already taken care of," she said.

Hunter dropped a generous tip on the table. "Now let's go."

Excitement thrummed through her, but Ali rationalized it was over the meal, not the man.

"But . . . I drove. My car," she said when they got to the lot.

"It's okay," he said. "You can ride over with me, and I'll swing you back by here after dinner."

Hunter opened the passenger door of a black muscle car. He must have noticed her hesitation. "It's okay. I'm a cop as well as your top student," he quipped. "You can trust me."

It's not you I'm worried about, she thought as she eased into the butter-smooth bucket seat. The car's interior smelled of leather upholstery mingled with the fresh, clean scent of his cologne. Hunter slid into the seat next to her, making her instantly aware of him in the car's confined cabin.

"Real food, here we come," he said, putting the powerful car into gear.

Ali usually passed a few restaurants touting down-home cooking on the short drive from her apartment to the school and back, but had yet to try one.

If the food at the place he was taking her to was as good as Hunter described, she'd be more than happy to forgo the processed frozen meals she ate on a regular basis.

"You cook?" Hunter asked.

"No," Ali said with a chuckle. "Spencer women may have many talents, but cooking isn't one of them. I can't cook. My aunt can't cook, but don't tell her that, and neither could my grandma. My dad used to say it's a curse."

Hunter laughed aloud as he eased the car to a stop at a red light. "So, what does the man in your life think about that?"

An awkward silence ensued.

"Hey, sorry about that," he said. "I didn't mean to pry."

"No, it's okay. I'm divorced," she said. "My ex-husband and I ate out a lot."

Ali gazed out of the window, as the brightly lit busy streets gave way to subdivisions with cookie-cutter houses flanked by tree-lined streets and manicured lawns.

"Where are we going? I don't see any restaurants around here?" She felt foolish for not asking the question sooner.

"We're here." He pulled in front of a brick ranch-style house. Two SUVs were parked side by side in the driveway, while two kid's bicycles and a trike were strewn haphazardly on the postage-stamp lawn.

Ali stiffened in the passenger seat.

"But I'd assumed we were going to another restaurant," she said. "I just can't barge in on people I don't know."

"Yes, you can." He came around and held open the passenger-side door. "You're with me, so just consider yourself among friends."

Still, Ali was apprehensive about walking up

to a stranger's door at dinnertime empty-handed
and looking for a meal. Her aunt would be ap-
palled if she could see her right now.

The front door of the house opened before
they made it halfway up the drive, and three
little boys charged toward Hunter shouting his
name.

"Hey, guys," Hunter said. He rubbed the older
boys' heads and tucked the smallest one under
his arm like a football.

A harried woman, dressed in a denim skirt,
T-shirt, and Crocs, came to the door, a dish towel
in one hand and another anchored on her hip.
"Boys!" She barked the word like a drill sergeant
to new recruits. "Stop climbing all over Hunter
and go wash your hands for dinner."

"Aww, Mom," the biggest one grumbled, reluctantly releasing his grip on Hunter's pants leg.

"And get those bikes off the grass and in
the garage where they belong," she added.
"N.O.W."

"What does that spell?" the youngest one
asked as Hunter set him back on his feet.

"Now," the middle kid said resignedly, up-
righting a red bike with training wheels and
rolling it toward the garage.

With her boys doing her bidding, the woman
turned to Hunter. Her eyes twinkled as her
pretty, ebony face broke out in a huge smile. "Just
in time for dinner," she said.

"Pete taunted me with your pot roast all day long."

"That's why I always make plenty. And I see you brought company," she said, smiling at Ali.

"Ali Spencer, this is Sandy Jameson. She's my friend and coworker Pete's wife, and the little guys putting away their bikes are their sons."

"Glad you came, Ali. As you can see, I'm outnumbered. It's always good to have another girl around. Come on in."

"Are you sure this isn't an imposition?" Ali asked, still uncomfortable with the idea. "I know you weren't expecting an extra mouth to feed."

"It's no problem. My Crock-Pot and bread-making machine did all the work." The woman looped her arm through hers, and Ali willed her body to relax.

As deep as the wound her husband's cheating had made, in some ways the betrayal of her best friend hurt more. Not to mention the friends who'd abandoned her once the tabloids printed those lies.

The episode had not only made her wary of other people's intentions, but it made her question her own instincts as well.

Oblivious of her hesitation, Sandy pulled her in the direction of the house. "It's good to see Hunter out with someone new, but you didn't have to get all dressed up," she said in a low voice meant only for Ali's ears.

"But we're not—"

"Pete," Sandy yelled for her husband, cutting Ali off. "We've got company."

Chapter Six

Hunter saw the sidelong glance Sandy exchanged with her husband and knew he had to set them straight.

He should have made it clear there was nothing romantic going on between him and Ali the moment they'd arrived, but the smell of real food had hit him as soon as he'd walked through the door and they'd all been too busy stuffing their faces to talk.

Also, the couple's boisterous boys had kept them entertained throughout the meal with meandering stories and jokes with forgotten punch lines.

"Then Nate squirted juice through his nose," one of the boys said, sending his brothers into guffaws of laughter.

Sandy smiled at their antics and shook her head, before turning her attention to him and Ali. "So, how long have you two been seeing each other?" she asked.

Her question caught him with his mouthful of dessert.

"Oh, it's nothing like that," Ali said.

"Ali's new in town," Hunter explained. "I was bragging on your cooking. When I found out she'd been existing on frozen dinners, I took the liberty of bringing her along."

"So, how'd you two meet?" Sandy asked.

"He's my student," Ali said before he could answer.

A puzzled look creased Sandy's brow. "Student?" She looked across the dining room table at him. "Pete never mentioned you were taking a class. What are you studying?"

"Aw, man," Pete groaned.

"Just a little self-improvement course," Hunter said hurriedly in an attempt to save his friend's bacon.

"Yeah, no big deal," Pete added, jamming a huge forkful of cake into his mouth.

Sandy arched one eyebrow and leaned forward. "So, Ali, what do you teach?"

Ali gave Hunter a questioning glance, before turning to their hostess. "Etiquette. Hunter's one of my new students," she said.

Instantly, Sandy yanked her elbows off the table and smoothed the paper napkin on her lap. "Boys, stop licking your fingers and use your napkins," she hissed at her sons, who continued to happily scoop up the creamy white icing with their fingers and stick them in their mouths. "And sit up straight," she added to no avail.

Sandy turned her attention to her husband. "You see what kind of example you're setting for the boys?"

"For goodness' sake, Sandy. We're at home, not having tea with the queen."

"That's no excuse for bad manners, right, Ali?"

Ali smiled. "Your boys are delightful," she said diplomatically. "Dining with them has been a pleasure."

Hunter was impressed at how his instructor sidestepped the question, as if she hadn't heard the burp contest the boys had started but their mother had put a stop to before they could declare a winner. Still, Sandy was shrewd, and he didn't expect her to buy it for a second.

But to his surprise, she brightened at the compliment.

"So, Hunter, what made you take an etiquette class?" Sandy asked. "And don't give me any of that self-improvement nonsense."

"It was Erica's idea." It was the first time her name had come up since he'd arrived. Moreover, it was the first time he'd thought about her all evening.

Guilt prickled at him although he hadn't done anything wrong. He and Ali had a professional relationship. They weren't even friends. Not really. He glanced at his instructor, who was sipping the coffee Sandy and Pete had brought out to accompany the cake.

Sandy frowned, her expression filled more with pity than disapproval. "So, is Erica still trying to kick down locked doors with her checkbook?"

"She'll come around," Hunter said, feeling like a politician repeating the same tired sound bite. Judging from the expression on his friends' faces, it had about the same effect as political verbiage.

He was surprised when Ali interjected, "I've only had a brief glimpse of Erica, but I think having you on her side makes her a very lucky woman."

Ali's words rang sincere, but her voice held a bittersweet note as she continued. "Loyalty is a very important quality in a partner."

Touched by the heartfelt support of a woman he hardly knew, Hunter thanked her with a barely perceptible incline of his head. Again, he wondered what kind of a man was responsible for the sadness lurking in the depths of her soft brown eyes.

Had it been the ex-husband she'd clammed up about after mentioning on the ride over?

Hunter felt a hand cover his. It was Sandy's.

"I don't mean to come off so harsh. It's just that we worry about you." She glanced over at her husband, who cleared his throat.

"So, Ali, what do you do when you aren't teaching folks not to eat with their feet?" Pete asked.

"I can eat with my feet. Wanna see?" one of the boys piped up.

Both Hunter and Ali laughed at the long-suffering look Sandy shot her husband, and he looked over at his sons. "Don't even think about it, fellas."

The boys' disappointment didn't stop them from holding out their plates for seconds on the delicious but rapidly disappearing cake.

"Actually, the school itself has kept me pretty busy. It's an old building and it's fallen into disrepair over the years," she said.

"Ali's been doing a lot of the repairs herself," Hunter interjected, feeling a flicker of pride.

"Wow, I'm impressed," Pete said. "What kind of repairs?"

"Just simple fixes so far. For example, this week I finished replacing all the ripped screens and broken windowpanes, and the other day I installed a motion-detector light. I've been reading about the rash of home burglaries in the paper, so I thought the light would be a good idea."

"Well, if you run out of things to do over there, I could use a hand around here. Between my crazy work schedule and keeping up with the boys, we've got a list a mile long of things that need doing around here I haven't had a chance to get to," Pete said. "And it costs so much to have someone come in and do the work."

Ali held up her hands, and Hunter noticed her nails were polished a pearly pink. "I've got more than I can handle right now."

Stifling a yawn, Hunter checked his watch. "It's getting late, and Pete and I have another long day ahead of us tomorrow," he said.

"Thank you both for a lovely evening," Ali said, rising from her chair.

"We enjoyed having you, Ali," Sandy said. "Boys, come say good night."

As the children practically attached themselves to him, Hunter felt a twinge of envy for Pete's life. He was a lucky man to have this kind of love.

An unexpected surge of longing hit, catching him off guard. He'd hoped he and Erica might find the same joy and fulfillment in raising a family.

"You'll be at my Little League game, right?" the oldest boy asked.

Hunter dropped his index finger on the boy's nose. "Of course I will."

"Are you going to bring your girlfriend?" the kid giggled, and pointed to Ali.

Hunter and Ali exchanged awkward glances, before he watched her turn away. "She's not my girlfriend, buddy. We're just friends."

"She nice," the middle boy said.

"And pretty," the youngest one of the brood chimed in.

Hunter's gaze flitted back to Ali, taking in her smooth caramel skin and glossy pink lips. He couldn't help noticing the kids had a point. She was nice.

However, they were wrong about her being merely pretty. Ali Spencer was beautiful.

The realization lingered in the back of his mind as he drove her back to the restaurant to pick up her car. And again he reminded himself he had absolutely nothing to feel guilty over. He was simply a man who noticed an attractive woman.

He switched the radio on. Not that Ali was the least bit interested in him anyway.

"I hope the home-cooked meal made up for the mess I made of our lesson," he said.

Jazz covers of hip-hop tunes played softly in the background as he steered the car through the quiet residential neighborhood toward the main artery that fed into the interstate.

"It was great," she said. "I know it's rude to go for seconds after showing up at dinner un-invited, but I couldn't help myself. Hopefully, I didn't embarrass you too badly."

"Honey, my face was buried too deeply in my own plate to notice."

She laughed and he took a moment to enjoy the melodious sound. The wall she'd erected around herself had slipped a few times tonight, and he'd caught her smiling at Pete and Sandy's banter or giggling at one of the boy's knock-knock jokes. To her credit, she didn't check anyone on table manners violations, and he was sure there were plenty of them. Instead she'd blended in seamlessly with him and his friends as if she dined with them every night.

He sneaked a peek of her in his peripheral vision. The hem of her dress had ridden up several inches, giving him a decadent eyeful of shapely thighs he knew led down to a pair of exceptionally appealing legs.

The car swerved, and he forced his attention back to the road. He gripped the steering wheel tighter as if it would help him get a hold of his wayward thoughts.

"Thank you for bringing me along tonight," she said. "It's been a while since I've enjoyed a meal with other people. . . ." Her voice trailed off.

"Glad you enjoyed yourself."

He glanced toward the passenger seat and saw her staring out of the window.

"Your friends really care about you," she said.

Sadness tinged her tone, making him wish there was something he could say or do to make it go away.

"I'm sure your friends back in Florida miss you too," he offered.

"They weren't my friends."

They rode the remaining minutes to the restaurant in silence.

"It's the red Honda," she said as he pulled into the parking lot.

The lot was more crowded than when they'd left with European luxury sedans taking up nearly every space. Hunter slid into the first open spot he could find.

"Wait," he said, when he saw her go for the door handle.

Rounding the car, he held open the passenger-side door. "I may not know the difference between water and sherry glasses, but I've always known how to treat a woman."

Ali jerked to her feet too fast and stumbled. Instinctively, Hunter reached out to steady her, and their eyes met. Heat sizzled where his hands touched the soft skin of her bare arms.

He inhaled the citrusy scent of her perfume as his gaze dropped down to her glossy pink lips.

Hunter knew he should take his hands off her. Instead he drew her closer. The streetlights illuminated her face in the darkness, and her eyes locked with his.

Hunter couldn't remember ever wanting to kiss a woman as much as he wanted to kiss this one.

A car horn blasted and Ali jerked back, breaking the spell she'd somehow weaved around him.

He opened his mouth to apologize to give her some kind of explanation for his behavior, but he didn't have one.

"Good night, Hunter." Ali practically ran to her car.

He simply stood there, his mouth agape, watching the taillights of her car fade into the distance. One thought echoed through his mind.

What in the hell just happened?

Chapter Seven

Ali muffled a yawn with her fist. Some professional you are, she thought, still disgusted at her behavior last night.

She'd thought arriving at the school early would get Hunter off her mind and make her focus on the busy day ahead.

However, visions of him and their near kiss continued to plague her as they had done to her restless dreams. Ali hugged herself, her fingers tracing the same spots his large hands had touched the night before.

"Oh, just stop it," she scolded. "You were all over the man. If you'd gotten any closer he would have had to zap you with a Taser."

Ali stalked over to her file cabinet, yanked open a middle drawer, and retrieved a stack of two-pocket folders. Plunking them down on her desk, she began stuffing the pockets with student material for the training program she was giving at a customer service phone bank this morning.

None of this would have happened if she hadn't left the restaurant with him, but at the time it had seemed so harmless. It had really been about the food.

Ali stuffed the last folder and pulled a sheet of labels embossed with the school's name in gold script from her desk drawer. She began affixing the labels to the front of the folders.

Unfortunately, the mindless task allowed her mind to drift, and it drifted right back to Hunter. For a moment she let herself savor the memory of his lips so dangerously close to hers and entertain the questions it brought to mind.

What if she hadn't pulled away? Would he have kissed her? And if he had, would it have been a whisper-soft brush of his full lips against hers or would his mouth have been firm and demanding?

Ali sighed as she stuffed the folders into her tote. She'd never learn the answers to those questions, because hooking up with Hunter or any other man was not on her agenda. Besides, his heart belonged to another woman.

She also could never pursue a man who was committed to someone else or respect one who cheated.

Shouldering her purse, she grabbed her tote and headed out the door. It was time for her to get her head where it belonged, on work.

Two hours later, Ali knew exactly why the customer service call center for Happy Home

Handymen needed her help. She stood behind a podium in front of a conference room table occupied by twenty disinterested customer service reps.

Her client had already indicated that the lackluster crew in front of her had been the best they'd been able to pull from their pool of applicants.

So Ali pasted a smile on her face and continued with the training program.

"People are already good and pissed off when they call here," a thirty-something woman with fuchsia hair and a pierced tongue said. "I don't care what you say about being respectful and addressing them as Mr. and Miss. It won't make a difference."

An older woman seated next to her nodded. "They're so busy complaining about having to wait two weeks for someone to look at their busted water heater or the repair guy botching the job, we can't get a word in."

"They're out for blood and ready to chew out the first person they get on the phone," a woman who looked to be the youngest said between loud cracks of her chewing gum. She'd been texting on her cell phone the entire time, so Ali was surprised she'd heard a word. "It's not my"—*snap*—"fault if they got fired"—*pop*—"are getting a divorce"—*snap*—"or whatever else they have going on in their life."

The nonstop gum popping set Ali's nerves

on edge, but she was determined to get through this presentation and, hopefully, get through to Happy Home's phone reps.

"Let's try something a little different." Ali walked from behind the podium. She picked up a phone from a back table and unplugged it, then asked the workers' supervisor for another one.

She set one of the phones down in front of the champion gum popper and glanced at her name badge.

She then held a sheet of paper under the young woman's mouth. "Jasmine, gum," she said simply, giving her a no-nonsense look.

Jasmine deposited the gum on the paper, which Ali balled up and threw in the trash.

"Okay, Jasmine, we're going to do a little role playing. I want you to pretend to be one of the more difficult customers you encounter," Ali said. "And I'll play the customer service representative."

Jasmine dived right into her role, blasting Ali with a long tirade. "Your guy stomps all over my carpeting with his dirty work boots, and now I've got to get someone else in to clean my damn carpet. So neither me nor my home are feeling very happy right now. Not to mention you showed up two hours after the supposed four-hour window you gave me. So, thanks to you people, I'm sitting here with grimy footprints on my white carpet, and I wasted a vacation day."

"First, allow me to apologize for your inconvenience," Ali said. She turned to the class. "Notice how I let the customer get it all out and not interrupt. It's important to hear them out."

Ali nodded for Jasmine to continue.

"Damn right it was inconvenient. We're talking about my hard-earned money here. I work hard," Jasmine said.

"I understand completely, Ms. Smith. Now let's talk about how we can resolve this matter." Again, Ali turned to the other reps. "Now that you've allowed them to vent, it's time to move them away from the problem and toward working out a solution."

"Solutions? We aren't going to pay them for the day or pay for their carpet," Jasmine said.

Ali turned to their supervisor. "If the complaint is legitimate, could you perhaps offer to send someone else out to clean the carpet for free and offer them another service at a deep discount?"

When the man hesitated, Ali reminded him how much it could cost him in bad word of mouth.

The supervisor nodded. "I guess we could do that."

She focused her attention back to the telephone reps. "Don't argue, stay calm, and stick to the facts," Ali said. "If the customer becomes profane or verbally abusive, they aren't going to allow you to help them anyway. Simply pass them along to a supervisor."

Jasmine sucked her teeth. "I just hang up on them."

"How angry would you be if the cell phone you've been texting all morning on was shut off, despite you paying your bill on time?" Ali asked.

"I'd be pretty mad."

"What would you want, a rep who listened and tried to make things right or one who threw the same angry words back in your face or hung up on you?"

"Well, if you put it that way . . ." Jasmine's voice trailed off.

"Thanks for your help, Jasmine," Ali said, then turned her attention to the group. "I know rudeness is rampant these days, but don't underestimate the power of good manners. It's all about dealing effectively with other people. Learn how and you'll be the one getting the raises and promotions on this or any other job."

The reps offered a weak applause at the end of her training presentation, but Ali wasn't sure if it was because she'd helped them or they were simply relieved it was over.

Still, deep down Ali couldn't help wondering if rudeness was too rampant or if maybe she was in the wrong business.

Hunter stood in front of the coffeemaker, mug in hand, waiting for the office sludge to finish brewing.

If he was going to clear his head of last night's

near miss with Ali, he needed something strong, black, and bitter. Even after adding an extra mile to his morning run, she lingered on the edges of his mind.

Filling his mug to the rim, he took a gulp of the toxic brew as if it were his punishment for coming so close to kissing another woman.

What had come over him last night anyway? He and Erica had their problems, but they were still in an exclusive relationship and committed to weathering this storm.

He didn't know where the overwhelming urge to kiss Ali had come from, but he rationalized it was a onetime thing.

He wouldn't let it happen again.

"Good afternoon, Prince Charming. Whatcha thinking about so hard?"

Hunter looked up to see his supervising sergeant with a shit-eating grin on his face. "Not you too," he groaned. "I'm going to kill Pete."

"Actually, Bishop mentioned how dapper you looked when you left last night. That charm school your girl has you in must be working, huh?" His boss chuckled as he filled his mug with coffee. "But do me a favor and don't mention it if you happen to run into my wife. I don't want to wind up being your new classmate."

A wisecrack about grown men being scared of their wives popped into his head, but he didn't need charm school to know pissing off his sergeant was a bad idea.

"So, did any of those leads on our burglars pan out?"

Hunter shook his head. "They've all been dead ends so far."

Just then, Pete approached them. He nodded at their boss before turning to Hunter. "We've got two more break-ins reported. On the same block, similar m.o. to ours," he said.

"Let's go," Hunter said. He was eager to see if interviewing the latest victims would turn up a good lead, or even better, if their suspect had finally slipped up and made a mistake they could use to their advantage.

Moments later, Hunter navigated the department-issued Malibu down Murfreesboro Road, while Pete adjusted the air-conditioning vents. "If spring is this hot, we're in for one miserable summer." Pete swiped at the perspiration dotting his forehead with his forearm.

"Yeah, I'm bracing myself for next month's electric bill," Hunter said. "I could have bought season tickets on the Titans' fifty-yard line for what it cost me to keep my town house cool last year."

Pete eased back on the passenger side. "Your place is just a few years old. Just wait until it gets a couple of decades on it like mine," he said. "Every time I turn around, something is on the fritz. Makes me wish Sandy was handy with a toolbox like your new squeeze."

Hunter's head swiveled toward Pete. "I told

you last night, Ali and I barely know each other," he said. "I'm still with Erica."

Hunter's words belied the images of Ali and that tempting mouth of hers playing through his mind. He felt as though if he inhaled he'd be able to smell the fresh, sweet scent of her citrusy perfume.

"Well, it didn't look like that to me last night."

Hunter slowed down as the yellow traffic signal changed to red. "She's my teacher, Pete. We're not even friends. Not really."

"I was there. I saw you, man."

For a split second, Hunter thought Pete had actually seen Ali in his arms. Not that it mattered. Nothing had happened between them, he reminded himself.

"I saw the way you were staring at her all through dessert," he said, and Hunter sagged in relief. "She was eating her cake, but you looked like you wanted to eat—"

"You're out of your mind." Hunter cut him off.

"I think you protest a bit much," Pete said. "And you looked relaxed for a change, like you were actually having a good time. When is the last time you had fun with Erica?"

Hunter successfully changed the subject by asking Pete about his oldest son's first season of Little League and the other boys' upcoming T-ball games. He knew once his friend started talking about his kids, he'd forget all about offering opinions on his love life.

However, Hunter hadn't forgotten Pete's last question. When was the last time he and Erica had fun? He didn't know what he didn't like more, the question or his unspoken answer to it.

"Make a left." Pete pointed out a tulip-flanked brick monument sign at the entrance of the Magnolia Cove subdivision.

Magnolia Cove, like the other communities their suspect favored, was brand-new. He estimated about half of the homes in the subdivision were occupied, with the rest in various stages of construction. Some of the roads hadn't even been paved yet.

Hunter braked to let workers behind the wheels of a slow-moving bulldozer and an excavator past him on the narrow gravel road. They followed the winding road until Pete spotted the street.

Pete pointed to a yellow two-story Cape Cod. "This is it."

They knocked on the front door and a thin, blonde woman peered at them through a sidelight window. Like anyone whose home had been violated, she looked visibly shaken. Hunter pulled his shield and identification from his pocket and held it up to the window for her to check.

A few moments later he heard the barrel bolt

slide, and she eased the door open. Hunter noted the splintered wood hanging onto the now useless dead bolt and glanced at Pete. The hollow-core doors and weak door frames the builder had used on these houses were no match for a crowbar.

"I'm Detective Coleman and this is Detective Jameson. We'd like to talk to you about what happened here, ma'am," Hunter said.

The woman stepped back to let them in. He looked down to see a toddler clinging to her leg. "Go play with your blocks while Mommy talks to the nice policemen," she said, then turned her attention to them.

"I was hoping you were the locksmith. They're coming out to fix the door and locks this morning. I'm also expecting the installer from the alarm company," she said.

"Good," Pete said.

"You also might want to consider a steel or solid wood door," Hunter suggested.

They asked her a few basic questions as she walked them through pristine living and dining rooms, filled with what appeared to be new furniture, toward the back of the house. "Like I told the officers who were here earlier, nothing was touched except our bedroom," she said.

Once they got to the bedroom, Hunter heard the woman's muffled sob. The room had been ransacked. Tossed clothing hung from open drawers and was strewn across the floor. Whatever could be broken was, including lamps, mirrors, and photo frames.

Hunter swallowed the lump of anger rising to his throat. He was mad as hell at whoever did this, but furious they hadn't been able to apprehend them yet.

He heard the sound of toddler footsteps coming their way, but Pete managed to stop the little girl before she entered the room filled with shattered glass.

"Whoa." Pete picked the girl up and handed her off to her mother.

"It's like they had radar," the blonde said. "They took all of my jewelry: two pearl necklaces, a diamond choker, and my great-grandmother's wedding band. They got the new leather briefcase I'd bought my husband for his birthday next week. It was hidden in my closet. I hadn't even had a chance to wrap it yet. Oh, also the gold Rolex and a fleur-de-lis lapel pin left to my husband by his father were also stolen. We've only been in here a few weeks. There was just so much to do, I didn't get a chance to go by the bank and put it in our safe-deposit box . . ." Her voice trailed off.

"Fleur-de-lis?" Hunter asked.

"A symbol usually associated with French monarchy. It looks like a flower with three petals joined at the bottom," she said.

Hunter shot Pete a questioning look.

"It's also the emblem on the New Orleans Saints football players' helmets," Pete said.

Well, why didn't you say so? Hunter wanted to ask, but refocused his attention to the victim. "Anything other than the jewelry?" Hunter asked the woman.

"We kept some cash in the house—six thousand dollars—you know, in case of emergency," she said.

"So, again," Pete said. "You were at work when this happened?"

She shook her head and readjusted the little girl on her hip. "No, that's the thing. My husband's away on a business trip, but I was just at the grocery store buying milk for Jennifer's cereal. I couldn't have been gone for more than a half hour."

After a few more questions, Hunter and Pete wound up the interview just as both the locksmith and the alarm installer arrived.

"Do you think we'll get any of our things back?"

"We'll do our best," Hunter said.

The second victim's house was only a few doors away, so they walked the short distance. "So, what do you think?" Pete asked.

"This guy is breaking in through front doors in broad daylight," Hunter said. "He's either a criminal genius or an idiot. Either way, we've got to put an end to his spree."

Hunter's cell phone vibrated. He glanced at

the number on the screen. Erica. So she was finally bothering to return his call from a few days ago. He started to let it go to voice mail, but decided to answer it.

"Oh, Hunter. I'm glad I caught you, sweetheart," she said as if everything was going great between them. "I've missed you."

"I've been here," he said, not wanting to get into why she'd been avoiding him in front of Pete, "but I'm working now."

"Are you free tonight?"

"Yeah, why?"

Hunter frowned as he listened to the real reason behind Erica's call, and he wished like hell he hadn't answered.

Chapter Eight

Ali rearranged the numbers she'd inputed into the bookkeeping program a third time, but the tallies remained the same.

The school was hemorrhaging money, and the small infusions of cash coming in hadn't been enough to stem the bleeding, let alone stop it.

She'd added five thousand dollars from her own meager savings to keep them afloat, but it wouldn't last much longer. The postman brought so many bills, her stomach began to hurt when he walked through the door.

Ali stared at the numbers on her computer screen until they began to dance in front of her, and then pushed away from her desk. She walked over to her office's sole window and stared out at the street.

Like the school, the neighborhood surrounding it had fallen on hard times. The recent brutal economy had turned storefronts that once housed flourishing small businesses to abandoned spaces.

Graffiti covered the building that used to be a flower shop, and sheets of plywood covered the broken-out windows. The bridal shop and furniture and office supply stores had met similar fates.

Now nail shops and convenience and cash-advance stores were the neighborhood's thriving enterprises.

The only exception was the coffee shop down the block. Voted the best coffee in Nashville three years in a row in both newspaper and television news surveys, it boasted a citywide customer base.

In fact, Ali suspected the proximity of the coffee shop to the school was one of the main reasons some parents had enrolled their children in her classes. They could enjoy a caffeine break while she transformed their rambunctious offspring into little ladies and gentlemen.

Ali drew in a deep breath and exhaled. She went back to her desk and stared at the numbers again, hoping a miracle had occurred and the sums were no longer in red.

"What are we going to do?" she asked the computer screen.

She crossed her arms over her chest and massaged her shoulders with her fingertips, but she couldn't rub away the tremendous burden on them. Images of her aunt Rachel and the photos of generations of Spencer women who had come before them lodged themselves in her brain.

While Ali's stint at the school would only be temporary, if she failed she'd be letting them all down, and she couldn't let that happen.

She closed the bookkeeping program and opened up a file of ideas she'd been brainstorming.

Somehow she had to make it work.

Having no one else to turn to, Hunter knocked on the door of the one person he thought would be able to help.

Ali jerked up from her laptop screen. "Hunter?" She frowned. "I thought our next class wasn't until tomorrow night."

"It isn't, but I needed to see you." His immediate crisis overrode any awkwardness he felt at seeing her again after nearly mauling her in the restaurant parking lot.

She quickly closed the lid of her computer and stood. She wore a short-sleeved sweater in the Pepto-Bismal shade of pink she favored, and gold earrings in the shape of palm trees dangled from her ears. Just the sight of her made him smile inside.

"Of course, come in."

"It looks like you were busy. I can come back another time."

"Don't be silly. You're here now." Ali gestured for him to have a seat as she sat down, but he preferred to stand. He paced from one end of her office to the other before stopping in front of her desk.

Hunter blew out an exasperated breath. "She wants me to go with her to the opera. Tonight."

Ali's shoulders relaxed, and the concern on her face melted into a grin. So much for him thinking she'd be the one person who wouldn't laugh.

"I shouldn't have come here." He turned on his heel. "Sorry to bother you."

"No, wait. I'm not smiling because I think it's funny," she said. "I think it's wonderful."

"What?" Hunter asked incredulously.

"By your expression, I'll assume this will be your first opera? Did she mention the name of it?"

"*Tosca* or something like that," he said, finally sitting down.

"Ahhhh." Ali leaned back in her chair. "That's one of my favorites. Wow, I wish I were in your shoes."

"Yeah, me too."

She chuckled. "Opera's been the butt of a lot of bad situation-comedy jokes, but in reality it's good stories told through sweeping arias, lush melodies, and so much passion. The sets and the costumes are usually just as amazing as the spectacular voices."

Hunter watched her eyes soften as she continued the description. His gaze dropped to her glossed lips and he remembered how much he'd wanted to taste them the other night.

He shifted uncomfortably in his seat to conceal his growing hardness. What in the hell was going on with him? *You're with Erica,* he told himself. *She's the one you want.*

Now if only his brain could convince his body, which at this very moment only desired the woman in front of him.

Ali's voice took on a wistful tone. "It's really beautiful."

He cleared his throat as if the gesture would clear his head.

"Sorry for getting carried away," she said. "I'm a huge opera fan, and it's been a while since I've been to a live performance."

"Well, I'm more of a sports fan, and I'd rather be sitting in a stadium, dome, or field catching a game."

Ali flicked her hand in a dismissive wave. "*Tosca* is a great opera for a newbie. It has everything: love, lust, jealously, intrigue, deceit, even murder."

Hunter shrugged. "It's not like I'll be able to understand any of it. Erica mentioned it was in Italian."

"Don't worry, subtitles are projected above the stage so you can follow along. However, you'll probably be too enraptured in the performance to bother with them."

Hunter had to admit Ali's enthusiasm piqued his interest. He'd assumed tonight was more of Erica trying to make an impression on someone, but perhaps he'd misjudged her.

She could be as thrilled as Ali about it. Hell, if she was half as excited as Ali, she'd have a good time.

Pete's question returned to the forefront of his mind.

"When is the last time you had fun with Erica?"

If he kept an open mind about tonight, maybe they would have fun together again.

Ali lifted the lid of her laptop. "Let's see what we can do to help you out."

Her brow furrowed in concentration as she typed. "Ah, here we go," she said. "Lucky for you the Nashville Opera has a study guide on their Web site. Looks like it's chock-full of tidbits on tonight's performance."

Hunter heard the whirl of a printer in the background and moments later Ali handed him a printout of the guide.

"Read this over and you'll be fine. Also, the director is giving a talk, which will fill you in on some background, an hour before the performance. So if you can make it, I think it'll help you appreciate the experience," she said, returning her attention to the online version.

"Thanks for all the info. I feel a lot better than I did when I arrived."

Ali glanced at the computer screen. "Oh my God, it says the role of *Floria Tosca* will be sung by Enjolique Redmond. You are in for a treat. That sister sings like an angel."

"Sister?"

Ali nodded. "She's African-American. I saw her in *La Bohéme* last year in West Palm Beach, and she was amazing as poor, tragic Mimi. Oh, by the way, *La Bohéme* was also composed by Puccini. There's a short bio on him in the print-out I ga . . ." she paused. "I'm getting carried away again, aren't I?"

"A bit, but I appreciate your help," he said.

"No problem. I can hardly wait to hear what you think of it."

"Looking forward to it," Hunter said as he left her office. And he was indeed looking forward to seeing her again, more than he had a right to.

Ali wasn't sure which was more pathetic.

Sitting at home alone thinking about Hunter and his gorgeous girlfriend enjoying their opera date or roaming the mall alone looking at clothes she couldn't afford, wishing she were there with him.

She'd thought a shopping trip, even if it was only window-shopping, would cheer her up.

It hadn't.

Ali flipped through a rack of skinny jeans with two-hundred-dollar price tags. A year and a half ago, she would have been shopping with her best friend and assistant, Kay, and she would have thought nothing of buying a pair for both of them.

Now she was too broke for pricey jeans and too jaded to let another woman get close to her.

Ali stalked out of the store into the mall corridor. Maybe she couldn't afford new clothes, but she could drown her sorrows in a giant cinnamon roll.

She paused by the directory to see if she was headed in the right direction.

"Ali, is that you?"

Ali braced herself and forced a smile to her lips, prepared to greet one of her students' mothers. She turned toward the voice and was surprised to see Sandy.

She smiled, genuinely happy to see her.

"Doing a little shopping?" Sandy asked.

"No, just looking," she said. "And I want to thank you again for dinner last night."

"Girl, please." Sandy waved a dismissive hand. "We were glad to have you, especially me. It was nice not eating with just the boys for a change."

Ali laughed. "And your sons are adorable. I enjoyed meeting them." She looked around. "Are they here in the mall?"

"No way," Sandy said. "They're at home with Pete. I try to do a few laps around the mall a few evenings a week. My baby's two, and I still can't fit in my prepregnancy jeans."

Ali thought about how snug her clothes felt since she'd started mainlining chocolates. "I do need to do something."

Sandy nudged her arm. "There's no time like the present. Walk a lap or two with me."

"Okay." Ali shrugged, figuring she really didn't need cinnamon rolls anyway.

They walked briskly down the long corridors, pointing out cute outfits gracing store window displays.

"When is the last time you could pull off something like that?" Sandy pointed to a skin-tight, strapless sundress that even made the mannequin look fat.

Ali laughed. "Never. I don't think the One-sies babies wear are that tiny."

Sandy sighed. "I used to go to the gym, but gave up my membership last year. I just never seemed to be able to make it over there."

"Tell me about it." Ali couldn't remember the last time she'd worked out regularly. "I used to run, but it's been so long."

"Really?"

Ali nodded. "I was training for my first marathon, but got distracted." More like the fact that she'd walked in on her husband screwing her best friend and her life imploded.

"Pete runs. Hunter too. But all that pounding the pavement isn't for me."

So Hunter was a runner, Ali thought as they continued walking. No wonder his body looked so incredible. She thought about how she'd braced her hands on his powerful biceps the night she'd stumbled. Her fingers had itched to roam up to his wide shoulders and feel their way down his broad back.

Good Lord, she needed something, all right, and it wasn't more chocolate or a cinnamon bun. Her attraction to Hunter had reminded her how much she missed being held, touched, kissed, and having a man make love to her.

As if on cue, Sandy asked her about him. "I know we don't know each other very well, but I was curious about you and Hunter."

"There is no me and Hunter. He's a client." She averted her eyes from Sandy's penetrating gaze. "Why on earth would you think anything else?"

"Because I saw the way you looked at him when you thought no one else was looking, and the way he looked at you."

"Well, you're wrong," Ali said, walking faster. "Hunter has a girlfriend that looks like she belongs on a magazine cover, and who at this very moment he's taking to the opera."

Sandy didn't appear convinced.

"Besides, I'm much too busy with my work at the school to get romantically involved," Ali said.

Sandy stopped midstep. "Speaking of work, there's something I wanted to ask you."

Grateful for the change of subject, Ali felt the tension ease from her bunched-up neck and shoulders. "Let me guess, you want to enroll your boys at the school."

Sandy shook her head. "Don't get me wrong, they could use it, all right, but that's not it."

"Then what is it?" Ali asked her, curiosity piqued.

"I was wondering if you could show me how to replace my kitchen faucet."

Chapter Nine

Hunter sat riveted as Enjolique Redmond's rich soprano commanded the theater, bringing fiery diva Floria Tosca to life.

Enjolique's celestial tones along with the classical tenors, baritones, and basses making up the rest of the cast touched a place deep inside him with their heart and powerful voices.

Ali had been right when she called it moving, he thought. Subtitles scrolled across a screen above the stage, but he didn't want to look away from Enjolique's expressive chestnut-hued face to read them.

Now he understood Ali's love of the opera, and her eagerness to help him enjoy it. He wished she were seated beside him in the darkened theater so he could witness her passion for it firsthand.

Erica drowsed, and Hunter cringed inwardly as a snore rippled down their aisle. Several people turned in their seat, and he didn't have to see their faces to know they were glaring.

Hunter nudged her with his elbow.

"What?" she snarled, her voice husky with sleep.

He inclined his head toward the performers, not wanting to cause more of a disruption by whispering in her ear as she was mumbling as she came out of her sleep.

Erica yawned audibly, not bothering to stifle the noise with her hand.

Hunter heard a woman's voice hiss from down the aisle. He couldn't blame her. The performers' amazing voices had magically transported them back in time to early twentieth-century Italy, only to be yanked to reality by Erica's rudeness.

Hearing Erica's sharp intake of breath at the admonishment, he placed his hand over hers to forestall an outburst and to try to reconnect with her on some level.

The evening had gotten off to a bad start when he'd arrived at Erica's penthouse wearing his charcoal suit instead of the tuxedo she'd wanted.

"You promised to make an effort," she'd whined.

The fact that he was even going required major effort on his part, he'd wanted to say, but kept a lid on it to keep the peace. They needed a pleasant evening out together.

"My date should be wearing a tux," she'd said. "You never know who we'll run into."

He'd kissed her lightly on her heavily made up cheek. "No one will be looking at me," he'd said. "You look good enough for both of us."

"I do, don't I?" Erica had twirled to show off her shimmery gold cocktail dress. It had a deep slit up the side to highlight her long legs.

In the darkened theater, Hunter kept his hand over Erica's until the curtain dropped on the opera's first act and the lights came on.

"Is it over?" Erica asked. "Thank God."

Then why did you pretend like coming here tonight was so important? he wanted to ask but didn't bother. He already knew the answer.

"It's just the end of the first act," he said aloud. "We have twenty minutes, so let's go out to the lobby to stretch our legs a bit. I believe they have champagne."

A smile overtook the scowl marring her thin face. "Now you're talking."

They made their way to the crowded lobby. Two of the Tennessee Performing Arts Center's four venues had performances that evening, and the opera audience flowed out into a lobby already jammed with people there to see the repertory theater's new show.

"I believe you mentioned champagne," Erica said.

Fortunately, Hunter was able to slip into a short line and retrieve two glasses. He took a sip of the bubbly, wishing it were a cold beer instead.

"Don't look, but Mrs. Palmer and her husband are coming this way," Erica whispered excitedly. "She's a former ambassador to some wretched country in the middle of nowhere and very tight with Vivian Cox."

Hunter blew out a breath. Again, with Vivian Cox. He didn't know what he was sicker of, hearing the woman's name or Erica's all-out campaign to impress her.

"Mr. and Mrs. Palmer, how lovely to see you here."

Hunter turned as Erica greeted a tall, regal woman with a huge smile. The woman wore a simple black dress and her graying braids were swept atop her head. Mrs. Palmer and her husband returned Erica's exuberant greeting with tight smiles that didn't reach their eyes.

"I see you're awake now," Mrs. Palmer said.

Hunter watched Erica's smile falter. "I . . . uh . . . I wasn't asleep. I just prefer to enjoy the performance with my eyes closed so I can fully appreciate the singers."

The other woman studied Erica a moment, the corner of her mouth pulled upward in a nonamused smile. "I'm glad you could appreciate it, because it didn't seem as though it could keep your attention."

Mr. Palmer, who reminded Hunter of a grim-faced undertaker, nodded his bald head. "Sounded like somebody was riding a Harley up the aisle," he muttered.

Hunter told himself he wasn't going to butt in. Besides, this time wasn't like the other occasions when the people Erica was desperate to impress took potshots at her. The Palmers, along with everyone sitting in their section, had a legitimate gripe.

"How could someone doze through such a moving story? I don't understand." Mrs. Palmer continued while Erica stared on helplessly.

Hunter hadn't intended to intervene, but his girlfriend looked so pitiful. Biting back the urge to tell them they'd made their point and to get off her back, he tried another approach.

"I was told the singing of *Te Deum* was a highlight of the first act, and I wasn't disappointed. What did you two think?" Hunter directed his question at the Palmers.

"I tell you I was sitting on the edge of my seat." Mrs. Palmer clasped her hands together in front of her chest. "The baritone gave me the chills."

Her husband bobbed his head. "We had the opportunity to hear him sing last season in *Don Giovanni*. Mesmerizing."

"This is my first opera," Hunter admitted. "I read in the study guide *Vissi d'arte* is also a noteworthy aria."

"Oh yes," Mrs. Palmer enthused, and went on to point out what Hunter should listen for in the second and third acts.

The lights flickered, signaling the end of the

intermission. Mrs. Palmer turned to Erica. "It's not often you come across a man so cultured and handsome. You're a lucky woman," she said.

His girlfriend's plastered smile lasted until the Palmers were out of earshot.

"I don't believe you did that," Erica said, the scowl returning to her face.

"What? Come to your rescue?" Hunter asked incredulously as they walked back into the theater.

"All you did was make them fawn all over you and make me look stupid," she hissed.

"I thought I was helping you. Besides, I tried to get you to come early to hear the director's background lecture, but you claimed to know all you needed to know about this opera," Hunter shot back.

"You didn't have to show me up with all that talk of arias and tenors and whatnot."

Hunter scrubbed a hand down his face, unable to believe what he was hearing. He'd preached patience to Sandy, Pete, and everyone else Erica had offended since she became wealthy, but she finally had him on the verge of losing it.

"You're the one who wanted me to be 'charming.' Isn't that what the classes I'm taking for you are all about?"

"Well, maybe they were a mistake. You're becoming too charming for my tastes."

The auditorium lights dimmed as they took their seats. Despite the tension between him and Erica, Hunter found himself sucked into both the second and third acts of the performance. Meanwhile, Erica fumed beside him with her arms crossed over her chest.

He rose to his feet clapping as the actors came out to take their bows. The applause grew thunderous when Enjolique Raymond took her last bow and the curtain fell a final time.

Tension followed them like an overhead storm cloud on the short drive to Erica's penthouse. He pulled up to the curb near the entry to her building.

"I was out of line back there," she said finally. "I'm sorry."

"It's okay," he said with a sigh.

She laid a hand on his arm. "Do you want to come up?"

He shook his head. "It's been a long day. I need to get to bed."

"That's exactly where I want you."

She crossed her legs suggestively, letting the slit of her dress fall open, revealing her thigh. His mind flashed back to Ali sitting in the passenger side of his car, and how a glimpse of her shapely thigh had practically set his mouth to watering.

Ignoring her invitation, he rounded the car and opened the passenger-side door for her. "Maybe another time."

Realization dawned on Hunter as he drove to his town house. He wanted to get in a woman's panties tonight, all right, but that woman wasn't Erica.

It was Alison Spencer.

Erica couldn't believe it. Hunter had turned her down.

She stalked through the foyer. An overhead crystal chandelier illuminated the pricey art and antiques along the corridor. The real estate agent had said it was decorated with an eye for European modernism. Erica just knew it looked expensive, in keeping with the image she wanted to project.

Usually, she marveled at the posh décor, still unable to believe she lived in such a grand place. She also wished her mother, a housekeeper who'd spent her life cleaning up after rich people, were alive to see it.

Tonight, however, she was oblivious of her surroundings. Erica's ears were peeled for the sound of Hunter's footsteps coming up behind her. When she didn't hear him, she glanced over her shoulder.

No Hunter.

Erica stopped. She pivoted on her Christian Louboutin pumps and looked through the glass door. His car was gone.

He'd actually gone home to his dinky town house rather than spend the night in her luxurious penthouse with her. Even after she'd swallowed her pride and offered up an apology, when it was clear she hadn't done anything wrong. Not to mention hinting she wasn't wearing anything beneath her dress.

She bit back another wave of disappointment. It wasn't going to happen tonight.

Raising her chin, Erica walked past the concierge station. It was Hunter's loss. Anyway, she didn't like how he'd made her look bad in front of the Palmers.

"I was told the singing of Te Deum was a highlight of the first act," she mimicked.

Then he had admitted to them this was his first opera like some ignorant bumpkin, rather than letting them believe this was a typical outing for them.

Erica exhaled, the thought of it angering her all over again.

Yet she knew once she'd had him in her bed, she would have been more than willing to forgive him.

"Good evening, Miss Boyd."

The concierge walked from behind his desk and used his key to open the elevator leading to the penthouse level.

"You look lovely tonight. Did you enjoy your evening out?"

Erica exhaled sharply as she boarded the elevator. "I'm not in the mood for small talk tonight, Dan," she said crisply. "Just take me up to my floor, please."

"Yes, ma'am."

Guilt niggled at her. She shouldn't take her foul mood out on Dan. It wasn't his fault she was stuck riding in the elevator with him instead of Hunter. If fact, she'd given Hunter a key to the elevator when she'd first moved in. Back then he couldn't wait to get her alone in the elevator.

She heard a chime and the doors opened. Erica pulled some bills from her clutch and offered them to Dan to make up for snapping at him.

Dan kept his hands at his side. "No, thanks, Miss Boyd."

Damn, Erica thought. Was every man in Nashville turning her down tonight?

Inside her penthouse, she kicked off her shoes and poured herself a glass of wine. She downed it in one gulp and helped herself to another.

She walked over to the floor-to-ceiling windows, which offered a spectacular view of downtown Nashville.

"I'm on top of the world, literally," she said, hoisting her glass in mock salute to the sparkling city lights.

Then why did she feel so miserable?

Erica took a generous sip from her wineglass. Her mother had dreamed of one day living like the people she'd cleaned up after and shared her fantasies of the glamorous life with her daughter.

Gladys Boyd would pick her young daughter

up and twirl her around. "One of these days, a rich man is going to take one look at my beautiful little Erica and make her the queen of one of these castles," she'd say.

Gladys had scrubbed toilets to put her Erica through nursing school, and after graduation she secured her daughter a private-duty job taking care of a wheelchair-bound woman.

Erica had grown very close to her wealthy, elderly patient over the years, more so after Erica's mother had suffered a fatal heart attack. Neither of them had family, so their bond had been like one of blood relatives.

Erica circled her finger around the rim of the near-empty glass. Her patient's death six months ago had been a heartbreaking blow, but she was shocked to learn the woman had left her the bulk of a considerable estate.

Now she was finally the queen of the castle, as her mother had always wished, Erica thought. Unfortunately, her subjects hadn't realized the old Erica was gone forever.

Vivian Cox had yet to give her stamp of approval that would guarantee Erica access to the best clubs and committees and acceptance among her elite social circle.

Then there was Hunter, who was doing absolutely nothing to help her toward her goal. If anything, he'd become a hindrance.

Erica placed her empty glass on the table for

the maid to take care of in the morning and sauntered upstairs to her bedroom. Since Hunter Coleman didn't possess the kind of charm and sophistication she required in a partner, maybe it was time she found a man who did.

Chapter Ten

Ali arrived at the school early again the next morning, eager to begin her day.

After walking around the mall with Sandy last night, she still hadn't wanted to go home to an empty apartment. She'd thought about stopping by her aunt's house, but vetoed the idea. It had been nearly nine o'clock at night, and more than likely, her aunt would have been asleep.

So instead she'd stopped by a twenty-four-hour, big-box home improvement store on her way home from the mall. There was so much the school needed, she didn't know where to begin. However, after scouring the aisles for the better part of an hour, she'd decided on a portable air-conditioning unit, and at the last minute she'd tossed a new ceiling fan for her aunt's office into her cart.

Although Aunt Rachel got around better than a person half her age, Ali realized she was getting up in years. She wanted to make her aunt's office more comfortable this upcoming summer,

because who knew when they'd be able to afford central air-conditioning?

Ali walked into her aunt's office, intending to
install the fan before the older woman came in
to work, but was surprised to see her aunt already seated at her desk.

"Aunt Rachel, I didn't expect to see you here
so early."

Her aunt looked up from the papers she'd
been reviewing and greeted her with a smile.
As usual, she was wearing a suit, in a flattering
shade of lavender. "I wanted to get this paperwork done before my 'Art of the Afternoon Tea'
class," she said. "I'm going out to lunch today."

Ali raised an eyebrow. "With a man?"

"You know better," "Aunt Rachel responded
with a smile. "I'm having lunch in Franklin with
my friend Vivian. We pledged sorority together
back in college," she said. "Since your uncle
passed, the only man in my life is Jesus."

Her aunt's husband had died before Ali was
born, but there were framed photos of him in
nearly every room of her aunt's home.

"That reminds me," Ali said. She grabbed a
chair from across the room and plopped it
down in front of her aunt's desk. "Edward and
I went out for coffee," she said.

"Oh." Her aunt averted her eyes as she re-
shuffled the sheaf of papers in her hand.

"Don't you want to hear about our date?"

Ali narrowed her gaze. "The one you insisted I go on."

Her aunt put down the papers and sighed. "Alison, I didn't know. Really, I didn't. When Celia bragged about her newly single nephew, she implied he was your age. I had no idea he was older than me."

"How did you find out?"

"Celia brought him by the house after his date with you. He wanted me to use my influence to convince you to go out with him again."

Ali's mouth dropped open. She shook her head to get the horrific thought of Edward and his *magic pills* out of it. "I hope you're not going to try, because there's no way I'm going out with him again."

"Certainly not," her aunt huffed. "I told him to put on some proper clothes, take those asinine earrings out of his ears, and grow up."

"You didn't?" Ali asked with amusement in her voice, wishing she could have been the proverbial fly on the wall.

"Yes, I did. Then I told him to go home and beg his wife's forgiveness."

"Good for you, Auntie," Ali said. She leaned forward in her chair. "Do you think he'll go back to his wife? Do you think she'll take him back?"

Aunt Rachel rolled her eyes. "I don't care."

She lowered her voice and winked. "I just don't want that old goat to wind up being *my* nephew."

Ali threw her head back and laughed until tears brimmed in her eyes. She looked over to see her aunt laughing too.

"I'm sorry for practically forcing you into that blind date," Aunt Rachel said. "You're welcome to start your techie or whatever you called it class with my blessing."

Ali shook her head. "Oh, it's going to take more than that to get you back in my good book."

Her aunt dabbed at the tears of laughter in her own eyes with a handkerchief before blowing out a defeated breath. "What do you want?"

"I need you to promise me that you won't try interfering in my life again," Ali said. Once the embarrassment of this attempt wore off, she didn't want her aunt playing amateur matchmaker again.

Her aunt looked down before raising her head to meet her gaze. "I'm afraid I can't do that, dear."

Ali sighed. "You know how much I adore you, but I simply can't allow you to interfere in my life again."

"It's too late," he aunt said. "I've already stuck my nose into your business."

"Oh, Auntie," Ali groaned, wondering what the older woman had obligated her to do now.

"I mentioned to my soror, Vivian, that you lost your job at that paper down in Florida. Long story short, she pulled a few strings."

Ali watched her aunt pull open the top drawer of her desk and take out a business card. "An interview has been set up for you at the paper here. Here's the managing editor's card." She slid it across her desk. "He's expecting your call."

"I can't," Ali said with determination. "Any job I get will be on my own merits."

Her aunt shook her head. "This is simply an interview, dear. If a job comes out of it, believe me, it will be on your own merit."

Ali took the card and slipped it into her pocket. She rounded the desk and hugged her aunt. "Thank you, Auntie."

A strange feeling enveloped her as she walked down the hallway toward her own office. It took her a few moments to realize it was *hope*.

She hadn't felt it in a very long time.

Hunter smoothed his hand over the section of drywall and ran the sandpaper over it again. He'd spent the other night scraping off the worn cabbage rose print wallpaper from his grandmother's old dining room and patching the dings he'd made in the walls.

Today was his first day off in two weeks. He planned to spend the morning sanding down the rough spots from his patch job and prepare the walls to paint.

He pulled his dust mask down and walked over to change the station on the satellite radio he kept here to keep him company while he worked. The soulful sounds of an R & B song gave way to the strains of the opera channel. He turned up the volume.

Hunter had no idea who the singer was or what the song was about. All he knew was he liked it.

"Who do you think you're fooling?" he muttered, covering his nose and mouth with the mask. He picked up the sandpaper again. "You like it because it makes you think of Ali."

Visions of the joy on her face when she'd tried to prepare him for last night's performance floated to the forefront. She'd been so excited over the opera, she'd lowered the invisible wall she'd erected around herself, and for a little while she'd let him in.

It made him wonder what it would be like if she really dropped her guard around him. His thoughts drifted to the kiss they'd nearly shared.

Hunter rubbed the sandpaper harder against the wall. He had no business entertaining those thoughts. Although it hadn't seemed like it lately, Erica was the woman in his life.

He thought about the way she had acted last night. He'd done his best to help her, and she'd basically had a hissy fit. Even if he had followed her up to her place, nothing would have happened between them.

Her behavior had been a total turn-off.

A knock sounded and the front door squeaked opened at the same time.

"Son, is that you?" his father's voice called out.

Hunter yanked down his dust mask and sighed. He hadn't wanted to get into this yet, especially with his father. "I'm in the dining room."

The senior partner of the corporate law firm bearing his name, Michael Coleman was usually at his downtown offices or in court at this time of day.

"What are you doing here, Dad?"

His father, in his workday uniform of dark suit, white shirt, and paisley tie, looked about the room in amazement as he walked on the drop cloth covering the floor. "I thought the same thing when I passed by and saw your car parked in the driveway."

"Careful," Hunter said, getting between his father and one of the walls. "You don't want to get dust on your suit."

His father sidestepped the wall. "Thanks." The shocked expression remained on his face. "I have a meeting with the chief executive officer at the hospital."

For as long as Hunter could remember, his father's firm had handled legal matters for the community hospital just a few blocks away. His father continued to look around. "I had no idea you've been working on Mama's house."

Hunter swallowed hard to push down the remorse that still rose to his chest at the mention of his grandmother. Fifteen years had passed since she'd died, but Hunter's guilt lingered.

Ignoring the dust, his father ran a hand over the walls. "I see you took down the wallpaper," he said.

"A few days ago." Hunter hesitated. "Are you okay with it?"

Although the house belonged to him and he didn't need his father's permission, the old man's approval was still important. He was relieved when his father smiled.

"I begged your grandmother for years to let me take it down, but she refused. Your grandfather had put it up as a surprise for their first wedding anniversary, and she didn't care how old and ugly it got, it was staying."

Hunter remembered his grandmother standing in the same spot he was standing on now saying the very thing. The thought of her standing with her hands on her hips defending the hideous wallpaper brought a smile to his lips, even if he couldn't manage a laugh.

His father slapped him lightly on his back. "No, son. I don't mind. Mama's been gone a long time now," he said. "It's time."

"I'm going to paint in here." Hunter rubbed

his hands against his work jeans. He went to the other side of the room and retrieved a color sample card. "What do you think?"

His father eyed the shades of terra-cotta and scanned the room. "It's going to be quite a change, but a good one, I think. It'll give the place a masculine feel to it."

"I already pulled up the carpet. The hardwood floors underneath it are too nice to hide. I'm planning to sand and refinish them."

"Do you need a hand? I put myself through undergrad working construction. Even at sixty, I can still pound a mean hammer. I could come by on the weekends."

Hunter shook his head. He'd turned down his father's offers over the years to renovate the old house. He'd even refused his father's more than generous offer to buy it from him.

"I can't explain it. All I know is it's important for me to do the work on this place myself. . . ." Hunter paused and smiled briefly at his father. "But I appreciate the offer."

"I can't wait to see how it turns out." His father inspected a section of wall Hunter had already sanded smooth. "So, are you thinking of moving in here when you're done?"

Hunter shrugged. "I don't know," he answered truthfully.

"Son, you have to forgive yourself. I know your grandmother wouldn't want you beating yourself up like this."

Hunter stiffened. "Not now, Dad."

His father threw up his hands in mock surrender. "Okay, I'll let it go, but your mother will have my hide if I don't ask when you're going to come by the house for dinner."

"Soon," Hunter said, relieved his father had dropped the subject. "Now come see what I did with the kitchen."

His father stopped midstep and glanced at the radio. He raised a graying eyebrow. "Opera?"

Hunter smiled. "It's a new interest of mine."

Ali hummed a tune from *Tosca* as she stood on the ladder positioning the last blade on her aunt's new ceiling fan. She'd been floating on the sliver of hope her aunt had given her since this morning.

While having an interview was a long way from being a columnist again, thanks to Aunt Rachel and her friend Vivian, she was a lot closer than she'd been yesterday.

Moreover, figuring out a strategy for the upcoming interview with the paper's managing editor kept her from fretting about seeing Hunter again tonight.

Ali heard a deep male voice hum in tune with hers, and she turned toward the doorway. Leaning against the doorjamb of her aunt's office, looking sexier than any man had a right to, stood the man she'd been trying not to think about all day.

He was early, she thought, taking in the slim black jeans and gray silk T-shirt. She wanted to run her hands over the ultrasmooth fabric of his shirt and feel the hard body beneath it.

"I could have used your help today over at my grandma's old place," he said.

Genuinely happy to see him, she smiled before she could stop herself and began climbing down the ladder. "Sorry, but Sandy already has dibs on me. I'm helping her install a new kitchen faucet tomorrow."

He walked over to steady the ladder and she found herself dangerously close to him by the time her foot touched the bottom rung.

An easy grin spread over his face, his white smile contrasting against his smooth brown skin. She breathed in his shower-fresh scent and willed her knees not to go limp.

Ali cleared her throat. "So, how is that project coming along? You were redoing the kitchen, right?" Still her voice sounded unnaturally high, as if she'd taken a hit from a helium balloon.

Hunter released the sides of the ladder and took a step back, giving her some much-needed space. "No, the kitchen's complete. I'm working on the dining room walls."

Ali walked over to the wall switch. She'd already checked the motor on the new fan, but wanted to see the blades in action. She flicked on the switch, and they began to rotate.

"Feels cooler in here already," Hunter said, looking up at it.

"Give me a moment to ditch this tool belt, and we can get started with your lesson," she said. "But first I want to hear all about last night."

Hunter's brow creased. "Last night?"

Ali unbuckled her tool belt as she walked out of her aunt's office. "Your big opera date? I hope it wasn't that unmemorable."

He followed her down the corridor. "Oh, it was great."

"Did you get to show off your quickie opera crash course for Erica?"

His girlfriend's name felt awkward on her lips, but Ali had said it on purpose. It reminded her Hunter was in a relationship. There was little chance Erica or any woman would let a man like him go.

Ali stole a glance at him. Hunter was forbidden fruit. But that was the problem with something forbidden. It made you crave it even more.

"Yeah, Erica noticed," Hunter replied. His tone was dry and he didn't elaborate. Instead, he changed the subject. "Enjolique Redmond was everything you said and more. I couldn't believe all that voice was coming out of her petite body," he said, sounding like himself again.

"I know," Ali said. "I have a few of her CDs. You can borrow them if you'd like."

Hunter nodded. "I'd like that."

"Good, I'll make sure to have them with me when you come in for your next lesson."

"My last one."

Ali felt a lump of disappointment lodge in her chest. She'd known he'd only one lesson left. So, why did she feel almost blindsided?

She should be celebrating.

After all, she'd wanted to get his class over with as quickly as possible to put an end to this attraction she had to him. An attraction that seemed to intensify the more she got to know him.

"I know we haven't even started this one, but what's my last lesson on?" Hunter asked.

"How's your dancing?"

"I don't dance. Don't know how," he said.

"You will after your last lesson."

They turned into the room where Ali conducted lessons.

"Feels nice in here."

Ali inclined her heard toward the new portable air-conditioning unit, courtesy of the fat fee Erica had paid the school for Hunter's classes.

Guilt pricked Ali's conscience. The moment Hunter was in eyesight, she went from competent professional to a high school freshman with a crush on the captain of the football team.

Her thoughts drifted to her former best friend. Was this how Kay had felt about Brian? Had she been so overwhelmed by her attraction to Brian, she hadn't been able to stop herself?

No, Ali thought. There was no justification for what Kay had done to her, just as Ali couldn't continue to rationalize standing around drooling over another woman's man.

She wasn't on a date with Hunter. It was time she acted like the professional she was and did her damn job.

Ali stiffened her backbone and squared her shoulders, before facing him.

"I think we've had enough small talk this evening," she said in her very best all-business voice. "Let's get to work on those manners of yours."

Chapter Eleven

Hunter replayed yesterday evening in his head for the hundredth time. For the life of him he couldn't figure out what he'd said to make Ali change right in front of him.

How could a simple comment about a new air conditioner make her go from warm and friendly to ice cold in seconds?

He shifted in the hard, plastic chair as the commander's voice droned on in the background, basically repeating what they already knew.

The bottom line was the mayor had taken a bite out of the police chief's ass. The chief had taken a bite out of the commander's ass. And if the pinched look on the lieutenant's face was any indication, the commander had chomped on his.

Hunter had no doubt, if the shit kept making its downward spiral, he and the rest of the precinct's detectives would be missing sizeable chunks from their own behinds by the time the meeting ended.

What they needed was a break on this burglary case, he thought.

The guy had hit two more houses today. He and Pete had spent all day canvassing another new subdivision talking to victims, neighbors, construction and utility workers, but nobody had seen anything out of the ordinary.

Pete's chin dropped to his chest, and Hunter threw him an elbow to wake him.

"I miss anything?" Pete whispered groggily.

Hunter shook his head. Their commander, known for loving the sound of his own voice, continued talking. The monotone drone allowed Hunter's thoughts to once again drift.

Only this time he didn't think about last night's lesson on first impressions and party conduct. He thought about afterward, long after they'd said good night.

Ali had invaded his dreams. Erotic dreams where she'd dropped not only her guard with him, but her clothes and her inhibitions. He'd made love to dream Ali until his buzzing alarm clock had yanked her out of his bed.

Now he yearned for the real thing.

"Coleman. Bishop." Hunter heard his sergeant bark out his name, and straightened in his seat.

"Yes, sir," he and Bishop said in unison.

"You two mind snapping out of it and joining the rest of us or is there something more interesting in space?"

The sergeant didn't wait for an answer. "Coleman, fill the commander in again on what we know about these burglaries."

Hunter cleared his throat. "Sir, our suspect is bold. He or she walks right up to the residence in broad daylight and uses a crowbar on the front door. The homes so far have all had recessed entries so no one would be able to see anything unless they were looking straight on at the house. He's also fast," Hunter said. "And he always hits the master bedroom."

A few detectives nodded. Like Hunter, they knew most people stashed valuables in their bedrooms, making it the first place a thief looked.

"Sometimes he'll go for home offices and studies," Hunter continued. "Our suspect takes cash and expensive jewelry only, leaving behind the larger, big-ticket items. We estimate he's in and out in fifteen minutes, maybe less, leaving behind no fingerprints or clues."

"Witnesses?" the commander asked.

Hunter shook his head. "He sticks to new subdivisions in which the houses are in various stages of construction. Most of the victims don't even have neighbors yet," he said. "Also, because of the construction, there are all kinds of people in and out of the neighborhood all day long."

The commander nodded. "You guys stay on it. Meanwhile, I'm going to pull you some extra manpower from North Precinct," he said. "The mayor's office is fielding a lot of calls from nervous residents. So we need to find this guy and close these open cases."

The meeting ended about an hour after their shift, and Hunter and Pete made their way to the parking lot. "You got time for a beer?" Hunter asked.

Pete shook his head. "Headed to the ball field. Pete Jr.'s game is this evening." He looked at his wristwatch. "Started about the time the commander was getting his second wind."

Pete let out a huge yawn. "You're coming, right?"

Hunter remembered promising the kid he'd be there. "I'll meet you at the park."

First, he was going by the Spencer School, where he planned to ask Ali straight out about her sudden coolness toward him during their lesson. Hunter put his car in gear and turned out of the precinct lot. He would get to the bottom of it, all right, he thought.

He braked at a stop sign, and the reality of the situation hit him. What right did he have to barge into her office and demand to know where he stood with her?

Ali was being paid to coach him on etiquette, which left them acquaintances at best. Even though deep down it was beginning to feel like so much more.

He made a left turn in the opposite direction of Ali's school and headed for the ball field.

Talking to Ali should be the last thing on his

mind. He should be more concerned with Erica and the status of his real relationship. Although more and more it seemed as though he and Erica didn't have much of a relationship anymore.

Hunter found a parking space near the ball field. He stayed in his car a few moments before pulling out his cell phone and calling Erica.

He got her voice mail, again.

He snapped his phone shut without leaving a message. He'd track her down later. Meanwhile, except for his last class, he intended to keep as far away from Ali Spencer as possible.

"Pete owes me five bucks."

Ali watched as Sandy flipped the single handle of her new faucet on and off. Her face beamed like that of a kid tearing through a stack of birthday presents. "He insisted there was no way I'd crawl under the sink to install this baby." She ran a hand over the smooth brushed nickel. "Just wait until he sees it."

Finding Sandy's enthusiasm contagious, Ali couldn't help laughing. "You did a great job."

"Me?" Sandy said. "There was no way I would have figured it out without your help. Pete's been so busy working those burglary cases, who knows when he would have had time to install it? So, thank you, Ali."

They both jumped at the rumbling noise coming from the other end of the house. Sandy abandoned her new faucet and planted both hands on her hips. "Boys! Do I need to come in there?" she shouted in the direction of the melee.

"Noooo," a chorus of little boy voices sing-songed in reply.

Sandy turned back to Ali. "Now, where were we?"

"I was explaining that helping with the faucet was the least I could do after showing up for dinner uninvited the other night." Ali placed her basin wrench back into the pink and green toolbox her father had given her a few Christmases ago.

"You know that wasn't a problem. You're welcome anytime," Sandy said. "You got time for a cup of coffee?"

Ali hesitated a moment before accepting the offer. Sandy was the closest thing she'd had to a friend in a while. Her young students' mothers had made friendly overtures toward her over the last few months, but Ali had always refused their polite invitations.

However, mall-walking with Sandy the other day had shown Ali just how much she missed having girlfriends.

Ali took a seat at the kitchen table while Sandy rummaged around in a cabinet. She glanced at the stainless steel refrigerator, covered in children's artwork and fingerprints, and found herself hit with an unexpected wave of longing.

Every time she'd brought up the topic of kids

with her then-husband, Brian, he would put her off or change the subject. The next day or so afterward, he'd come home with some big surprise: a two-seater sports car or a tropical vacation; things designed for couples and not families.

Then he'd lost his job as a local television weatherman and their lives began a downward spiral.

"Dang it, we're out of coffee," Sandy said. "How about some sweet tea?"

"Sounds good."

Sandy pulled a pitcher of tea from the refrigerator and poured them both a tall glass. "An etiquette teacher who's good with tools makes you quite the Renaissance woman," she said. "Hunter mentioned your aunt owns the school, but how did you learn to be so handy?"

"My dad's a plumber. He took me wherever he went, and I picked it up along the way."

"Well, you're really good at it. Hunter said you were a patient teacher, but I saw it for myself today."

Ali thanked her, but was more interested in the fact that Hunter had been talking about her with his friends. She so wanted to ask Sandy what else he'd said about her, but she realized how juvenile it would sound.

I like Hunter. Does Hunter like me? What did he say about me?

She hadn't been that silly even back in high

school. Besides, hadn't she already decided to put him out of her head? They had one more session together. Then she'd deliver his girl-friend the Prince Charming she'd paid for, and the two of them could live happily ever after.

"Don't tell me you haven't considered it?" Sandy asked, pulling Ali out of her thoughts.

"I'm sorry, considered what?"

"Teaching do-it-yourself, or even better, do-it-*herself*, classes?"

"Not really," Ali said. She folded her arms on the table and leaned forward. "Right now, the school is struggling, and I've got my hands full trying to keep it afloat."

When she'd first come to Nashville, she'd only wanted to keep the place going because it was important to her aunt. However, spending countless hours in the building her ancestors had put their hearts and sweat into had made the school, that bore their name, important to her too.

"How can I help?" Sandy asked.

Ali shrugged and took a sip of tea. "I appre-ciate the offer, but I've tried almost everything I can think of—"

"Mom," a voice interrupted.

Ali looked up to see Sandy's sons standing at the kitchen entryway, one dressed in a baseball uniform.

"Coach says he wants us there early."

Sandy looked at her wristwatch. "Your game. I almost forgot."

Her son rolled his eyes. "How could you forget the game?"

Ali rose from her chair. "I'd better get going. Thanks for the tea."

"Hey, are you free in the morning?" Sandy asked. "The boys all have school. We can meet for coffee and brainstorm some ideas."

"I'd like that," Ali said. It would be nice to talk more about it with someone before broaching the possibility of having to close the school to her aunt.

"In the meantime, why don't you come with us?" Sandy asked.

"No, I—"

"Oh, come on," Sandy coaxed. "You can keep me company." Picking up on her hesitance, she added, "The park is a few blocks away. The walk will do us good."

Late afternoon sunshine and the scent of fresh-cut grass buoyed Ali's mood as she walked the five blocks to the neighborhood ball field. She took in the pops of color of the spring tulips and daffodils in the well-tended yards.

Neighbors waved in greeting as they walked past older but well-maintained homes.

Initially, Ali felt uncomfortable waving back, but after a few times her unease dissipated. Having lived in a condo for years and now an apartment, she'd forgotten how welcoming a real community felt.

The boys kept about a half block ahead of them, but waited on their mother's permission to cross the street.

"Hold your little brother's hand," Sandy called out to the older two.

An hour later, Ali was seated next to Sandy in the bleachers. Another mother with boys the same age as Sandy's had taken the younger boys off to play in the playground across the road from the ball field.

Sandy glanced at her wristwatch. "I wonder what's keeping Pete." She bit her bottom lip as she looked at the pint-sized ballplayers. "Pete Jr. will be up to bat again. I know he doesn't want to miss him."

"Is that him?" Ali pointed to a hulking figure headed toward the stands.

A huge grin spread across Sandy's face as she spotted her husband. She stood up and waved her arms. "Pete, over here."

Pete greeted Ali before squeezing his big body on the other side of his wife. "How's my boy doing?"

"*Our* boy has struck out twice, but he's up at the top of the next inning," Sandy said.

Pete's cell phone chirped, and he typed in a text message. "Hunter's here," he said. "I was just letting him know where we're sitting."

Ali's ears perked up at hearing Hunter's

name, and she tried to ignore the jolt of anticipation. Still, her heart turned a tiny backflip as
she watched him climb the bleachers.

She knew the moment he'd spotted her, because he'd stopped and his dark eyes widened.
He recovered quickly, his face an impassive
mask, as he stood at the end of their row. He
eyed the tight seating and looked to the rows
behind them.

"We can make room," Sandy said. She and
Pete moved closer together, and she gestured
to Ali to shift toward her.

Ali heard him sigh as he sat down next to
her. They'd just seen each other last evening,
so how come she felt awkward simply sitting by
him? And he appeared to be just as uneasy.

Their thighs touched. Ali's skin tingled
through her capri pants, and the still air around
them sizzled with electricity. She stole a sideways glance to see if he'd felt it too and found
him studying her intently.

Their gazes locked, and she watched his eyes
drop down to her lips.

"Come on, Pete Jr.," Sandy cheered.

Ali abruptly turned away from Hunter, breaking the pull of his magnetic gaze. How many
times did she have to remind herself to stop
lusting after him? Every day she gave herself
the same scolding, which seemed to go in one
ear and fly out of the other.

"You can do it, son," Pete called out.

Ali forced herself to keep her eyes on the children's game and off the man seated next to her. Even then the masculine scent of his cologne whispered to her, taunting her with the fact that he was off-limits.

The umpire called a second strike against Pete Jr., and Ali couldn't help feeling sorry for him as his small shoulders slumped in defeat. She crossed her fingers as he sidled up to the plate for another pitch.

"Remember what we practiced," Pete yelled. "See the ball. Hit the ball."

Pete Jr. glanced briefly into the stands and acknowledged his father's encouragement with an almost imperceptible nod. He swung, this time making contact with the ball. Ali cheered along with her new friends as their son's foot touched first base, and he was declared safe.

By the time the game ended, Ali was more than ready to go. While she'd enjoyed hanging out with Sandy and getting to know Pete, her proximity to Hunter had knocked her vital signs out of whack.

Ali felt her heart slamming wildly against her chest, while her pulse tapped out an erratic beat all its own.

Sandy gathered up her sons, who were walking toward their car with Pete. "Hunter, do you mind taking Ali back to our place for her car? We promised the boys pizza."

"It's okay. I can walk," Ali said.

"No, I'll drive you," Hunter said, a gruff edge to his tone. It was the first thing he'd said to her since he'd seen her seated in the stands.

Ali reluctantly accepted his offer. A few more minutes wouldn't hurt anything. At least, in his car they wouldn't be touching.

He held open the passenger door for her, and she slid past him to sit down. This was going to be the longest five-block ride ever, she thought as he started the engine.

They rode in silence until he braked for a stop sign.

"Did I say something to upset you before our lesson last night?" Hunter asked, finally breaking the silence.

"No, why?" Ali tried to sound casual, but her voice had an unnaturally high squeak to it.

"One minute we're having a friendly conversation, and the next you clam up on me." He continued to drive, but slower than the posted speed limit. "I thought we were on our way to becoming friends." He paused. "I'd like to resolve it if I can."

Ali chewed the inside of her lip. What was she supposed to say? *You've got me so hot that I think my underwear melted off.* Or maybe she should just straddle him on the leather driver's side bucket seat and ride him all the way home.

"No, we're fine." She counted down the blocks, relieved to see her red Honda parked in front of Sandy's house.

"I probably should have addressed this sooner," Hunter continued as he pulled up behind her car. "The other night when I . . . we almost . . . well, I didn't mean to offend you by getting too close outside the restaurant."

"Well, there's my car," she said, stating the obvious. She unbuckled her seat beat and bounded from his car. "I'll see you at your last lesson."

Chapter Twelve

Hunter sat in his car and watched Ali's tires practically burn rubber up the street. The arousal he'd battled sitting next to her on the park bleacher had turned into a full-fledged hard-on from the moment she'd sat in his car.

The soft scent of her perfume lingered in the enclosed space, summoning last night's dreams to the forefront of his thoughts. A lethal mix of sexy and sweet, Ali continued to haunt his every waking moment.

In his mind's eye, he could see her naked in his bed. Her soft lips starting a trail of butterfly kisses beginning at his throat and trailing all the way down to his . . .

A car honked in the distance, and Hunter gave himself a mental shake. He rolled down the window to clear his head, before driving off. He should be thinking of Erica. His girlfriend should be the woman he fantasized about all day and couldn't wait to get into bed at night.

Besides, he didn't like the way he and Erica

had parted the night of the opera, and it was time he'd remedied it. They needed to sit down and see where their dwindling relationship was going, if anywhere.

Pulling his cell phone from his pocket, he speed-dialed her cell phone number. Voice mail. He tried her house phone. No answer.

He tossed the phone into the car's cup holder. Erica was no doubt out somewhere bowing down to the almighty Vivian Cox, and Hunter wanted no part of it.

Nothing broke the ice like a big, fat check.

Erica watched the aging socialite's Botox-frozen face twitch upward in surprise and fought the urge to break into a grin.

"Oh my!" Vivian Cox clutched the check in her hand. "Aren't you generous?"

Erica dismissed the compliment with a wave, hoping the gesture gave the society maven an eyeful of the newest addition to her jewelry collection.

The ring, a two-carat Pigeon blood ruby encircled by diamonds, was a pricey but perfect complement to the scarlet silk organza gown she'd bought especially for tonight's Library Ball. Her publicist had snagged her an invitation. Now it was up to Erica to do the rest.

Appearances were everything with this crowd, and if the expression on the grand dame's face was any indication, she'd finally made an inroad.

"On behalf of the foundation, I'd like to thank you. This will go a long way toward expanding the children's section and the adult literacy program." Vivian folded the check in half and stuck it inside her silver clutch. "Perhaps you'd like to become a volunteer?"

Caught off guard by the offer, Erica gaped at the older woman. Vivian wore a white Grecian-style gown accented with tasteful silver embellishments. Her mostly gray hair was swept back into a chignon held in place by a pearl-studded headband.

"I'll have to check my schedule," Erica said, careful to avoid committing herself. Volunteer? She didn't mind chairing a fund-raiser or contributing to a cause, but she had better things to do than bother with a bunch of bratty kids or people who should have learned to read in elementary school like everyone else.

She steered the conversation in another direction. "As you know, I've applied for membership to both the Ladies' Lunch League and the country club. I expect they'll both keep me busy."

Vivian looked down at her platinum watch. "Goodness, where's my mind? I have to check on the champagne."

"But I was hoping to talk to you about my—"

"Sorry, dear, but I must make sure there's enough bubbly to go around."

"But . . ."

Vivian disappeared in a whiff of Jo Malone fragrance before she could say another word.

Erica realized her mouth was still hanging open and pressed her lips together hard to keep from screaming in frustration. Damn it, she had as much money as anyone in this room. Yet the town's upper crust continued to look through her.

She glanced around the room. Crystal chandeliers illuminated the opulent ballroom, and couples danced to the orchestra playing in the background. Feeling excluded from the laughter and conversations surrounding her, she toyed with the idea of giving up her quest to become part of this world.

Images of her mother kept Erica's feet rooted to her spot on the marble floor. Her mother had dreamed of this life for her, and damn it, she was going to have it.

Erica squared her bare shoulders. She'd just have to find another chance to corner Vivian before the evening ended. Erica needed to be sure of her support.

Snatching a flute of the champagne from a waiter bearing a silver tray, Erica downed it in one gulp. Good thing she hadn't brought Hunter along tonight. He'd shown her up at the opera in front of the Palmers, and she didn't want to take a chance on his making her look bad again.

She was especially glad he hadn't witnessed Vivian taking her check and running in the opposite direction. The last thing she wanted to see right now was an I-told-you-so look from Hunter.

It was one of the many disapproving looks he'd tossed her way lately, and she was getting tired of it.

Unfortunately, she hadn't tired of falling into bed with him, not that they'd done that lately. Her ego was still smarting from his rejection the other night.

"Looks like you could use another one."

Erica abandoned thoughts of Hunter, and her gaze followed the proffered glass to the man holding it. She took in the gold cuff links and flawlessly cut tuxedo. No, he definitely wasn't a waiter. Tall, trim, and undeniably elegant, this man belonged.

Erica accepted the champagne with a slight incline of her head. She'd noticed him earlier talking to the McAdamses, owners of one of the region's largest black-owned banks, and the Conways, who owned a string of luxury car dealerships throughout the state. He'd even brought a smile to the Palmers' lemon-sucking faces.

She took a sip of champagne, peering at him over the glass. He was attractive. Not in Hunter's blatantly sexy toss-me-over-your-shoulder-and-take-me way; his appeal was subtle. His presence whispered *wealth*, *privilege*, and *class*.

Though his smooth butterscotch skin gave no hints to his age, she estimated him to be over thirty.

Distinguished and classy, she thought. Getting to know him might open some doors that had been slammed shut in her face.

"Would you believe me if I said you're the most beautiful woman in the room?"

She was ready to laugh off the obvious line, when he caught her gaze and held it. His light brown eyes radiated sincerity.

"I might," she said with a hint of a giggle. Though she was not usually one to giggle or flirt, drinking on an empty stomach made her want to do both.

"In this sea of dull, basic black, you have the spirit to dazzle in red."

Erica had indeed noted the invitation called for guests to dress in black or white. Still, she'd chosen red to be noticed.

And she finally had been.

The smooth melodious lilt of his cultured southern accent dropped an octave. "I like it."

Erica's shoulders straightened at the compliment.

"By the way, I'm Taj St. John."

"Erica Boyd."

"Please to make your acquaintance . . ." He

paused to look pointedly at the bare ring finger on her left hand. "*Miss* Boyd?"

"Yes, it's still Miss."

"Glad to hear it." He glanced around them. "Now, where's the man I'm bound to upset by monopolizing your time this evening?"

"My date had an emergency tonight." She'd been stood up by Hunter's job so many times, the easy lie felt like the truth.

Taj smiled as if she'd just handed him the gift he'd been wanting for ages. "It must have been something big for him to leave someone who looks like you on her own."

A delicious shiver ran through her at the compliment.

"And where's the lucky lady with you to-night?" She managed to hide her excitement behind practiced nonchalance.

"I'm standing with her now."

"I find that hard to believe," Erica said. "You appear to be a man in demand."

He arched an eyebrow. "So you noticed me too?" Before she could answer, he added, "Those conversations were just business. Talking to you, so far, has been pure pleasure."

"So, what is your business, Mr. St. John?"

"Taj," he corrected. "Investments. I'm a personal finance adviser. And what is it you do besides dazzle at parties?"

She stifled her knee-jerk response of being a former nurse. "I'm a philanthropist."

Erica felt the most delicious buzz at saying the words aloud. Or maybe it was the champagne? Then she felt it again.

Her satin clutch was vibrating.

"Excuse me," she said, snapping open the purse and retrieving her cell phone. Hunter's name and number flashed across the tiny screen. She powered down the phone and stuck it back into her purse.

She'd finally met someone interesting, and she wasn't about to blow it talking to Hunter. More than likely, all he wanted to do was complain about the latest person she'd supposedly snubbed or insulted. He'd probably heard about her brushing Sandy and her mother off when she'd run into them downtown and was calling to make her feel guilty.

"Are you sure you don't need to call them back?" Taj asked. His liquid brown eyes stared down at hers. "It could be your date calling to make amends."

"Then maybe he should stew a bit," Erica said, meaning every word.

Taj extended his arm. "Dance with me. It would be a shame not to show off that beautiful gown on the dance floor."

Erica allowed herself to be swept up in his arms. Her cheek brushed against his jaw. She couldn't help comparing its clean-shaven smoothness to the stubble of Hunter's ever-present after-five shadow.

A woman of her status deserved to be in the arms of a charismatic man who effortlessly charmed people in high places.

Erica sighed and rested her head on his shoulder. The scent of his expensive cologne made her want to melt into his arms. He centered his hand on her lower back and drew her closer.

This was the kind of man she needed. One who could help her garner the recognition she deserved.

Chapter Thirteen

Sandy was already seated when Ali arrived at the coffeehouse, her hands wrapped around a cup brimming with froth and chocolate sprinkles.

"I overslept." Ali shrugged off her tote and took a seat on a plush velvet chair next to her. "Hope I didn't keep you waiting."

She left out the part about thoughts of Hunter keeping her up half the night. In reality, Ali knew he was hands-off, but in her dreams she could allow herself to imagine what it would feel like to touch him and finally give in to the overwhelming urge to kiss him.

By the time she'd finally drifted into a deep sleep, it had been time for her to wake up.

Sandy gave her a dismissive wave. "After the morning chaos of getting the boys up, fed, dressed, and off to their various schools and preschools, it feels good to just sit here and breathe."

She took a deep sip from her coffee mug and eased back into her chair.

"So, how was pizza last night?" Ali gave her new friend a pointed look.

"Was I that obvious?"

Ali nodded. "You practically pushed me into the car with the man."

Sandy sighed. "I know, but when I see you two together, I can practically see the sparks flying off you. All you need is a little shove in the right direction."

Ali shook her head. "It's not going to happen, Sandy. Hunter has a girlfriend, and from what I can tell he's very much in love with her."

"It's not love." Sandy rolled her eyes skyward. "I've seen them together, and the light he used to have in his eyes when he looked at her dimmed a long time ago." Sandy leaned on the arm of her chair toward Ali. "Now the only time I see Hunter's eyes light up is when he looks at you."

Ali shook her head. Sandy was mistaken. Hunter had barely said a word to her at the game last night, and he hadn't looked pleased to be stuck sitting beside her.

"Ali, I believe Hunter fell out of love with Erica a long time ago," Sandy continued. "All he really feels for her now is loyalty."

"Loyalty?" Ali broke her struggle to appear blasé.

"Hunter cares about Erica. He doesn't want her money and ambition to get her into trouble,"

Sandy said. "But that's a long way from being in love with her."

Ali tried to quell the hope bubbling up in her chest. Sandy was wrong, she told herself. Besides, even if she wasn't, Hunter was still in a relationship. Ali would never do anything to interfere. No matter how she felt about him.

"Aren't you having coffee?" Sandy asked.

"I'll grab some in a bit," Ali said.

Silently, she reminded herself she hadn't met Sandy to talk about Hunter. "Actually, I'm eager, make that desperate, to brainstorm some ideas with you for the school," Ali said, changing the subject.

Sandy straightened in her seat and placed her drink on the table beside it. "Well, I already called the mothers with sons in Little League and Cub Scouts with my boys," she said. "And I tell you, they were thrilled at the prospect of transforming their monsters into little gentlemen. I only wish I could enroll Pete along with the boys. He could do with a brush-up course on table manners."

Ali couldn't help smiling at her new friend's conspiratorial tone.

"We cover more than just dining etiquette. My boys' classes also cover telephone manners, good sportsmanship, and grooming. Even the proper way to tie a necktie."

"I'll pay you double if you manage to accomplish all of that with mine," Sandy said.

"That won't be necessary," Ali said. "And thanks."

Sandy waved her off. "I wish I could have come up with something more helpful," she said. "Anyway, you should be hearing from some of the mothers soon. I know a few boys won't be enough to get the school back in the black, but it's a start."

"I'll just have to figure out a way to build on it," Ali said. "And to tide us over financially."

"Have you considered taking out a business loan?"

Ali groaned. "I don't think there's much chance of a bank granting us a loan in the current economic climate. Not with our declining revenues," she said. "However, I do have a job interview at the local paper. If I land it, I plan to plow the bulk of my salary into the school."

Ali felt Sandy's hand on her arm. "Good luck, but I'm sure you won't need it. Who wouldn't want to hire someone like you?"

"Thanks," Ali said, feeling genuinely touched by the gesture of friendship.

Still, deep down, she couldn't help wondering if their efforts would do any good. She was starting to feel as though an etiquette school in the twenty-first century was much like the building housing the Spencer School: hopelessly out of date.

"Oh, are you mall-walking today?" Ali asked, hoping some physical activity would brighten her perspective. "You've inspired me to start getting in shape."

Sandy shook her head. "Not today. I have to drive my mother to a doctor's appointment later."

Ali nodded. "Okay, maybe another time."

"But there's a park that Pete runs in that has a trail," she said. "You may want to check it out."

"Thanks, I think I will."

Guilt warred with annoyance as Hunter pushed open the entry door of the thirty-story glass and steel tower that housed Erica's downtown penthouse.

He'd tried calling her again this morning, and his call had gone directly to voice mail. However, they couldn't put off having a long, serious talk about their relationship.

Hunter knew he should have made it his business to come down here sooner, but he'd rationalized he was giving her the space and time she needed to get this social climbing business out of her system.

Who are you kidding?

It had been out of sight, out of mind.

Ali had unwittingly crowded Erica out of his head, and perhaps even out of his heart. Although they'd never kissed and he'd only made love to her in his dreams, he still felt guilty as hell.

Erica's wealth might have made her arrogant

and inconsiderate at times, but she wasn't the bad guy everyone around him seemed to believe. Deep down, she was still the compassionate, down-to-earth woman who had cared for her longtime patient as if she were family.

Moreover, she'd always been forthright and faithful. She'd earned his loyalty.

Hunter walked past the foyer and down the corridor leading to the elevators. Knowing his longtime girlfriend, she was probably still in bed with the covers pulled over her head. He'd put on a strong pot of coffee when he got upstairs. They needed to figure out if the differences ripping them apart were permanent or if they could somehow be mended.

"Morning, Detective Coleman."

The building's concierge's greeting roused Hunter from his speculation.

"How's it going, Dan?"

Hunter considered running into Dan one of the perks of coming to Erica's building. An avid sports fan, Dan could talk ball twenty-four-seven. Whether it was football, basketball, baseball, or golf, Dan could recite the latest scores and highlights.

"Pretty good." Dan rounded his command-center style desk and gave Hunter's hand an enthusiastic shake. "Haven't seen you around much lately. Have you been camped out in front of the tube watching games too?"

"Games?"

Dan narrowed his eyes. For a moment, Hunter thought he was going to put a hand on his forehead to take his temperature.

"The NBA play-offs and baseball's season openers, of course," he said. "What's the matter? They working you too hard down at the cop shop?"

"I haven't even had a chance to catch up on the scores," Hunter admitted.

"Oh, did I mention signing my granddaughter up to play T-ball this year?"

Hunter smiled despite the turmoil going on inside him. "She any good?"

"Is she any good?" Dan repeated incredulously. "Just yesterday, we were in the backyard practicing and she hit the ball over my fence. Only four years old. I'm telling you, she's a natural."

Hunter felt the tension in his shoulders ease a bit at Dan's lighthearted banter. Still, he was anxious to hash things out with Erica.

He pulled his key ring from his pants pocket and singled out the two accessing the penthouse elevator and her door.

Though Hunter had his own keys, Dan liked to ride up to the penthouse floor with him to squeeze in more sports talk.

"So, what do you think about the Titans next season?"

"I don't know, man," Hunter said. "The offense looked like crap last season, and the defense wasn't much better."

The two men played amateur football coach, each tossing out ideas on how he'd improve Tennessee's NFL team until the elevator chimed, and the doors opened on Erica's floor.

"If only the real coach listened to us," Dan called out as the doors closed behind Hunter.

There were three condos on penthouse level. He heard the faint sound of Erica's laughter as he approached her door.

He exhaled deeply. At least she was awake.

Unlocking the door, he knocked before pushing it open. "It's me, Erica," he called out, so as not to startle her.

"Hunter, wait!"

The warning came a second too late.

Hunter stepped into the living room, and he felt his body go cold.

He scanned the room slowly. An open bottle of champagne nestled in a bucket of ice sat on the coffee table beside two drained glasses. His gaze followed the trail of shed clothing, Erica's and a man's, leading up the spiral staircase toward her bedroom.

"Hunter! What are you doing here?" a naked and disheveled Erica stammered.

Finally, he turned to the woman he'd once considered making his wife. He forced himself to look at her. The faux hair stuck up all over her head. Her lipstick was smeared across her mouth, and she smelled heavily of sex.

Hunter watched wordlessly as she grabbed the ivory silk robe he'd bought her last Valentine's Day from the floor and wrapped it around her nude body. Her fingers fumbled as she tried to tie the sash.

Rage twisted through Hunter with the force of an F-5 tornado prepared to level everything in its path. He held his hands fisted at his side and closed his eyes in an attempt to gain control.

Dozens of questions flashed through his brain. The biggest one—how long had she been making a damned fool of him?

He exhaled as he opened his eyes, once again looking at her. He'd slapped handcuffs on too many scorned lovers who'd thrown their lives away for a taste of revenge. No, he wouldn't risk his career, embarrass his family, or lower himself to make a scene over her.

She wasn't worth it.

"Babe, what's taking so long?" a male voice called out.

Hunter looked up to see her buck-naked paramour standing at the top of the staircase.

"Go back into the bedroom, Taj," Erica said quickly.

The urge to run upstairs and smash his fist into the guy's face was strong, but Hunter held back. After all, this man hadn't cheated; Erica had.

He thought about the questions running through his head, but decided to forgo asking them. What could she say that would satisfy him or make him feel like less of a fool?

Nothing.

Hunter turned on his heel. It was time to put this scene and Erica in his past.

"Let me explain." Erica grabbed his arm.

Hunter felt something at his feet as he pivoted to face her again. He glanced down at the man's tuxedo jacket on the floor and roughly kicked it aside. A flash of gold on the lapel caught his eye, but Erica's steel-like grip on his arm distracted him.

He peeled her fingers from his forearm, her touch disgusting him. "No need," he said, the calm in his voice surprising even him.

"I'm sorry. We were at a party, and we had too much champagne. One thing led to another," she babbled. "He said I was pretty. He made me feel special. When is the last time *you* made me feel special?"

He turned on her. "When?" Hunter asked. "When I stuck up for you when everyone else was ready to write you off. When I let you drag me to all of those stuck-up parties. When I went to charm school to make you happy. When I stood by and let you make a fool of yourself trying to fit in with folks who don't give a damn about you."

He watched her flinch and her eyes narrowed.

"That's just it. Taj already fits in. He's polished, affluent, and classy." Her voice cracked. "With him, I can fit in too."

Hunter shook his head, finally seeing what everyone else had recognized long ago. The Erica he cared about was long gone, leaving behind this sad, shallow husk.

"I can't be angry at a woman who would sell herself so cheaply. I pity you."

"I'm sorry." She tried to reach for him again, but the look on his face apparently made her think better of it.

The sound of footsteps on the stairs caused them both to look up. Hunter noticed her lover had put on pants, but remained both barefoot and shirtless.

"Everything okay down here?" he said, avoiding eye contact.

The hairs on the back of Hunter's neck prickled, and the feeling of unease he got when he cornered a bad guy came over him. His instincts had rarely failed him, but Hunter couldn't rely on them this time.

After all, the man had just had sex with a woman Hunter thought he was in a relationship with.

Hunter's gaze flickered from Erica and back to her lover. "It's cool." He pulled her keys off his ring and dropped them on the side table. "She's all yours."

"Hunter, please," Erica called out.

He turned and looked at her one last time. "There are plenty of things I could say right now, but thanks to you I'm too much of a gentleman."

Waves of sadness and regret swamped Erica as she watched Hunter leave. She knew it would be a long time before she forgot the look of revulsion on his face.

It would take even longer for her to forget him.

She felt Taj's arms come around her waist from behind, and she closed her eyes to hold in the tears. Already she longed for Hunter's strong embrace. How could she have let a man she'd had the best sex of her life with walk out of her life for one she barely knew?

"I'm sorry you had to go through that," Taj said. "I'm sure it must have been difficult for you."

The idea of chasing Hunter down and begging him to take her back popped into her head. After all, she'd only cheated this one time. Before last night, she'd been totally faithful.

She dismissed the thought. Even if he would forgive her, and she doubted he could, it wouldn't change their ongoing problem.

Hunter didn't understand her desire to become one of the city's elite. She yearned to top everyone's invite list for the chicest parties and events, while he was happy at a backyard barbecue with Sandy and Pete. She wanted to serve on high-profile charity boards and committees, and he was content to serve a public that barely appreciated his efforts.

"Was he the one who stood you up last night?" Taj asked.

Erica nodded. "He's a cop, so he was always being called away," she said.

"Cop?"

Erica felt Taj's body stiffen, and he spun her around. "Did you say that guy was a cop?"

"A detective," she confirmed.

She briefly wondered why Taj seemed agitated, but waved off the thought.

Taj was so refined, Erica thought. A man like him had probably never witnessed a scene as ugly as the one she'd just gone through with Hunter. It had to have been hard for him too. She hoped it hadn't turned him off her.

"But that's over now," she said, both to herself and to him. Maybe Taj hadn't exactly rocked her world in the bedroom. He had what she needed outside it.

Taj pulled her close. "Come back to bed," he said. "I'll make you forget all about him."

Erica smoothed a hand against his jaw. Classy, good looking, and connected, this was a man who could help her achieve her dreams. With Taj at her side, she'd be the complete package. She'd no longer be on the outside of society looking in.

"Sorry, Taj, but that scene pretty much killed

the mood," she said, knowing another bout of below-average sex with him this morning would have the opposite effect.

"Perfectly understandable." His handsome face fell as he dropped his arms.

Erica sighed wearily. The last thing she wanted to do was hurt another man today.

"How about we order in some breakfast, and you can tell me all about how you know the McAdamses?"

Erica smiled to herself. Maybe she'd chosen the right man after all.

Chapter Fourteen

Hunter ignored the burning in his chest and his aching calves as his sneakers pummeled the hard pavement of the familiar park trail. He didn't care. He just wanted to run.

Run until it banished the tawdry scene he'd walked in on from his mind. Run until he didn't taste the bitterness of betrayal. Run until he didn't feel humiliated for stupidly believing in Erica long after everyone else had washed their hands of her.

He intended to run until he was too damn tired to think.

His sweat-soaked body began to give out on the twelfth mile, but the drumbeat of the how-could-I-have-been-so-stupid mantra continued to hammer in his head.

Hunter slowed his pace to a walk. This wasn't getting him anywhere.

Ambling over to the drinking fountain, he took a long pull of cold water. He cupped his hands, held them under the running faucet, and splashed water over his face.

He was relieved he had the day off. The last thing he wanted to do was face Pete and a host of others who'd tried to warn him about Erica.

The money had gone to her head, they'd said. It had changed her too much.

Now Hunter knew without a doubt, the Erica he'd seen this morning would never return to being the woman he'd cared about again.

Images of her answering the door naked and disheveled replayed in his mind. He splashed another handful of water over his face and braced himself for the onslaught of pain that usually accompanied heartbreak.

It didn't come.

Hunter stood, his hands still under the running water, as realization hit him full force. He wasn't hurting. The only thing Erica's escapade had wounded was his pride. His heart had remained intact.

"Hunter?"

Recognizing the familiar voice immediately, Hunter spun around.

Ali.

He took a moment to soak in the sight of her. Her face was scrubbed free of makeup, and her hair was pulled back in a low ponytail. She wore sneakers and a pink shorts outfit.

"Are you okay?" she asked.

"What are you doing here?" Hunter asked, surprised to see her.

"I don't have any classes today, so I thought I'd go for a walk. I have some things I'm trying to work out in my head," she said. "I've been watching you for a while, and you seem kind of out of it. Are you okay?"

Hunter smoothed away the concern creasing her brow with his fingertips as he pushed aside a lock of hair that had escaped her ponytail. "I wasn't, but I am now."

It was true. He'd felt better the moment he'd heard her voice. The sight of her was like sunshine breaking through the clouds after weeks of rain.

Hunter inhaled, drinking in her perfume floating on the late morning breeze. She grasped his forearm, and heat rippled through him. Her touch was soft and sweet just like the scent of her perfume.

"What happened?"

Hunter didn't want to talk about it. Not because it made him sad. Ali just seemed so far above the ugly scene he'd witnessed this morning.

He looked at her face again. The crease between her brows deepened, and he figured it would be worse to let her continue to worry. "I just left Erica's place."

"Oh?" She said, waiting for him to continue.

"She was in bed with another man," he said flatly.

"Oh, Hunter. No."

He looked deep into her eyes. Their depths brimmed with concern, tenderness, sympathy, and something else.

Empathy.

"Your husband cheated on you, didn't he?"

She abruptly snatched her hand away from his arm, and he found himself already missing her warmth. "How did you find out? What did you do, Google me?"

He shook his head. "I had no idea until this very moment. The look on your face told me."

"Yes, he did, so I've been in your shoes." Her chin dropped to her chest. "Only he cheated with my best friend. I don't know which betrayal hurt me more, his or hers."

Hunter touched his finger to her chin and lifted it until they were eye to eye. "Your ex is a damned fool."

"For what it's worth, I'm sorry this happened to you." Her voice was a husky whisper, but conviction filled the statement. It wasn't some platitude. She meant it.

Hunter shook head. "I'm not."

Ali's eyes widened. "How can you say that? You tried so hard to make it work, even suffering through my class."

He took a step forward until his face was mere inches from hers. "Because now I'm free to do what I've been aching to do ever since the night at the restaurant."

"What's that?" she asked, her voice barely audible.

"Taste you."

Without preamble, Hunter brought his arm around her waist and hauled her against his perspiration-soaked body. She gasped, and the lips that had taunted his dreams enticed him even more. The world around them fell away as he lowered his head and crushed his mouth to hers.

Hunter heard Ali moan as his tongue delved into her mouth.

The soft sound ignited the firestorm of longing he'd suppressed too long.

She wrapped her arms around his neck, returning his kiss with the same fierce hunger. Her hands grasped his shoulders, and she pulled him even closer.

He could feel the peaks of her breasts against his chest. Their delicious weight combined with the heady sensation of her sweet mouth nearly sent him over the edge.

Realizing they were in public, he forced himself to tear his lips from hers, ending the kiss long before either of them was ready. Still holding her against him, he stared down at Ali's flushed face. He felt the thump of her heartbeat as her chest rose up and down, her breath coming out in pants.

He dropped his head, until his forehead touched hers.

"Come home with me."

Ali knew there were at least a dozen good reasons why she should say no.

Hunter had just suffered a shock that had sent him into an emotional tailspin. He was on the rebound, and she didn't need the distraction of a man in her life right now.

The best thing she could do for him, for both of them, was to step back from his sweaty, sexy body and walk away.

Yet, as she stood with his arm wrapped around her and his powerful arousal pressed into her belly, all she could think about was satisfying the desire he'd stirred up the moment he'd walked through her door.

Ali shut her eyes briefly. *Do the right thing*, her conscience whispered. *Walk away*.

Finally, she raised her head until their gazes met, fully expecting to see the pain of another woman's betrayal in his eyes.

Instead, she saw a man who wanted her as much as she wanted him. One who wouldn't stop making love to her until she was calling his name in ecstasy.

"Yes, I'll go home with you."

Hunter's arm dropped from around her waist,

and he grasped her hand. His soulful brown eyes never left hers as he raised it to his mouth and bestowed it with the gentlest of kisses.

Ali's mind flashed back to the child who'd called him a prince. Now she knew the little girl hadn't been mistaken.

For now, Hunter Coleman was Ali's Prince Charming, and she could hardly wait for him to begin making her grown woman fantasies a reality.

He gave her hand a gentle tug and led her to his car. The air of anticipation thickened on the short drive from the park to Hunter's place.

Her mind could only focus on two tasks— getting him naked and getting him inside her.

Neither said a word, but he held her hand the entire ride, releasing it only when he turned into the driveway of a three-story town house and hit the garage door opener. He drove into the attached garage, and the door closed behind them.

Ali chewed on her bottom lip, both eager and nervous.

He opened the passenger-side door and pulled her to her feet. In an instant, she was in his arms. He kissed her hard and deep, leaving her breathless and weak. She sagged against him.

"Are you sure?" He inclined his head toward the door leading inside the town house. "Because once we're on the other side of that door, I don't think I'll be able to stop."

She slid her hand downward and palmed his impressive erection. "The only words you'll hear from me are don't stop." She squeezed his hardness as she rose on tiptoe to whisper in his ear, "Please. Don't. Stop."

"Oh God," he moaned.

He kissed her again, somehow managing to unlock the door to his town house without breaking contact with her lips.

Once inside, she didn't feel any of the curiosity or awkwardness at entering someone's space for the first time. She didn't care if he was neat or about his taste in interior design. Her only concern was how fast they could get naked.

Hunter grabbed the edge of his T-shirt and pulled it over his head, revealing his well-muscled chest and washboard abs. Her fingertips tingled as she reached out to touch him.

He grasped both of her wrists in one of his large hands and shook his head.

"Not here." He inclined his head toward a staircase. "Upstairs." His voice was half plea, half command.

They scrambled up the three flights, the last one ending in a huge master bedroom suite that took up the entire third floor. Her gaze fell upon the king-sized sleigh bed dressed with plush burgundy bedding.

She felt him behind her. He placed his hands on the sides of her arms and kissed her lightly on the side of her neck.

"I've dreamed of you in that bed," he whispered against her ear.

"What was I doing?" she asked boldly. The idea of him tossing and turning on that big bed thinking of her turned her on even more.

"Riding me."

Ali felt her knees buckle as the timbre of his deep voice turned her arms to gooseflesh.

"Cold?"

She shook her head. "No, just the opposite." She turned until she was facing him. "I'm hot to start making that particular dream come true."

Hunter reached for the top button on her shirt and unfastened it. She sucked in a breath as his hands brushed against the tips of her breasts while making quick work of removing her shirt along with the rest of her clothes.

His hungry gaze raked her from head to toe, lingering on her breasts, and she felt her nipples tighten under his scrutiny.

"You're beautiful." Hunter's voice, low and seductive, left her trembling with need. The day-old beard on his chiseled jaw scraped her skin as he began a series of slow kisses beginning at her neck and trailing down to her breasts. He lifted them with his hands.

"Do you know how long I've wanted to do this?" Without waiting for her answer, he flicked his tongue across one taut nipple and took it into his mouth.

He gently tugged it between his teeth, before giving her other breast the same rapt attention. "I knew you'd taste this sweet," he rasped.

Waves of pleasure washed through her and for a moment she thought she'd come right there. She pulled his mouth from her breasts and took a step back.

"I want to see you," she said. "All of you."

He ducked into the bath, and she heard the shower start. When he returned, he tugged both his gym shorts and briefs down over his lean hips. They dropped in a heap at his feet.

Ali barely noticed him stepping out of them or kicking off his shoes, her gaze transfixed by the sizeable erection calling to her from between his muscular legs.

"Like what you see?"

She licked her lips and swallowed hard, savoring him in his naked splendor. The sheer maleness of him took her breath away. Never in her life had she wanted a man so badly.

"It's been quite a while for me. I haven't since before . . ."

He stepped over to the nightstand and retrieved a large box of condoms from the drawer. "I've got all day with nothing to do but help you make up for lost time."

Again, her gaze fell to his erection. "Well, let's not waste it talking."

He pulled her into his arms and kissed her

soundly. Clothes no longer a barrier between them, Ali let her hands roam freely over his body. Her palms slid down the warm skin of his back until she was cupping his firm buttocks. She squeezed them as she ground against his thick length, reveling in the rock-hard feel of him.

Her feet left the floor, and she realized he had carried her into the bathroom. When the kiss ended they were both standing in the glass shower stall.

Steam rose as the warm water rained down on them. There was something deliciously intimate about being in the enclosed space with the man she'd lusted over for weeks, Ali thought. It was as if a fairy godmother had granted her sexiest wish with a cherry on top.

She reached for the soap. Water sluiced over them as she ran her slick hands over his hard chest, covering it in the fragrant lather. His amazing anatomy made her regret having only two hands. She'd yearned to touch him like this for so long. From his wide shoulders and powerful biceps to his broad back and tempting butt, she wanted to feel all of him—all at the same time.

"My turn." Hunter took the soap and rubbed it between his palms.

Ali's gaze met his, and the raw hunger in his eyes made her feel like the most desirable woman on earth.

"I'm going to touch every inch of you," he said, making her tremble in expectation.

Starting at her neck, he caressed her skin with his large hands, the slippery soapsuds heightening the sensation of his touch.

Ali gasped when he reached her breasts, taking his time with each one before replacing his hands with his mouth.

"Oh yes," she said, taking his head between her hands and holding it there. He alternated between breasts, each suck, lick, and gentle tug an exquisite torture.

Meantime, his hands continued their sensual exploration. They slid past her waist and over her hips until he reached the juncture between her thighs.

Ali sucked in a breath as his hand brushed against her swollen folds before he pushed a finger inside her.

"Hunter."

Ali opened her mouth, but her next words were smothered by his mouth. He kissed her long and deep, his tongue moving in tandem with his finger stoking the desperate need building within her until Ali thought she'd collapse from pure pleasure.

Heart-hammering, she pushed against his hard chest and pulled her mouth from his.

"Please," she gasped, her voice a hoarse plea.

Hunter removed his finger, and she fell back until her butt hit the shower wall. He leaned forward and braced his hands on the glass, one on each side of her head.

Lowering his lips, he brought them toward her ear as if he was about to confess his naughtiest secret.

"Please, what?" he asked, breathing hard.

She hooked a leg around his waist and pulled him close until his incredible hardness rested against her stomach. "I've wanted this so long," she said. "*Please* don't make me wait."

Ali shivered as Hunter stepped out of the shower, already missing the overwhelmingly masculine presence of his body. She heard the wrapper rip on a foil packet, and he returned to the steamy shower fully sheathed.

Hunter's hands slid down over her hips until he was lifting her butt with both hands. Ali grasped his wide shoulders and straddled him, wrapping her legs around his trim waist.

She closed her eyes in anticipation. She'd wanted this so badly for so long, and finally, it was hers for the taking.

"Look at me," Hunter huskily demanded.

Ali opened her eyes, meeting his hot gaze as he lowered her onto his erection. Her nails dug into his shoulder blades, and she bit down on her bottom lip to keep from crying out in joy as he filled her.

"So tight," he said in a broken whisper. "And so damned sweet."

Hunter stood motionless, and Ali knew he,

like she, was savoring the moment. Trying to prolong it, before animal instinct took over.

Then he began to move.

Ali's breath hitched as he thrust upward into her heat and pulled back. Deep and achingly slow. Each powerful movement sending ripples of pleasure pulsating up and down her spine.

Pinned between the shower wall and his body, she rode him, her pelvis rocking back and forth meeting his thrusts with her own. Her inner walls clamped down on him as he stroked her, squeezing him.

"God, you feel good," he rasped.

Ali opened her thighs wider and tightened her legs around him, forcing him deeper. He met her silent challenge by increasing the pace.

"Hunter." His name was a cry on her lips.

"Is this what you wanted?" he asked between pants as he stroked her harder, faster.

"Yes," Ali said breathlessly, her head rotating from side to side against the wet wall. "Oh yes."

The warm water pelted down on them as Hunter fulfilled her plea over and over again. The heat that had been building in her core exploding into waves of mindless pleasure.

A low growl tore from Hunter's throat and his body stiffened, before shuddering in its own pulsating release.

He held her as their heartbeats slowed to normal, and Ali knew she'd just had the best shower of her life.

Chapter Fifteen

Ali's dark lashes rested on her high cheekbones, and her sweet lips were curved into the
hint of a smile as she slept.

Hunter couldn't take his eyes off her.

He wasn't dreaming.

Ali's head was on his arm, and her gorgeous
legs were entangled in his sheets. Moreover,
he'd spent the better part of the day making
love to her. First in the shower and twice more
in bed, before pulling her into his arms and
falling into a deep sleep.

Hunter gently extricated his arm and managed to get out of bed without disturbing her.
Slipping on his robe, he padded barefoot
downstairs to the kitchen. He was starved and
expected Ali would be once she awoke.

Pulling open the refrigerator door, he scanned
the meager offerings. A trip to the grocery
store was in order. Until then, they'd have to
make do with bacon and eggs.

Hunter hummed his favorite tune from *Tosca*

while he cooked. With the toast down and bacon sizzling in the cast-iron skillet, he filled the coffeemaker with water and measured out a scoop of grounds.

Footfalls sounded on the staircase behind him, and he paused.

"Did I wake you?" he called out over his shoulder as he cracked open a few eggs and added them to the pan.

"No, the bacon did. I could smell it from upstairs."

He turned around, and his next breath caught in his chest. Although he'd spent the better part of the day with Ali, the sight of her made him smile.

She looked beautiful.

The silky hair he'd sunk his fingers into when he'd pulled her in for kissing fell to her shoulders in tousled waves. He was glad she'd left it down. His gaze traveled down to the threadbare denim shirt from his closet. Despite the sleeves rolled up to her elbows, it was huge on her.

"I borrowed your shirt. It looked like an old one. I hope you don't mind."

He abandoned the stove to kiss her lightly on the lips. "I've never seen that shirt look better."

"It smells delicious in here. Can I help with anything?"

Hunter divided the bounty between two plates.

"I was going to bring this to you in bed, but since you're here . . ." Before he could finish his sentence, she turned tail and began walking up the stairs. "Hey, where are you going?"

"If I have a shot at a near-naked man serving me breakfast in bed, then I'm not missing it." She looked back at him over her shoulder. "Even if it is dinnertime."

Hunter watched her hips sway as she slowly climbed the stairs. He remembered how those sexy hips had rocked against his, and he felt his groin tighten.

Lord help him, he wanted to bury himself inside her all over again.

Hunter managed to push the images of how they'd spent the afternoon out of his head long enough to pour coffee and take a tray upstairs.

Having cleaned her plate, Ali proceeded to devour the last of his toast as Hunter looked on. Afterward, she rolled her eyes heavenward, leaned back on the headboard, and patted her stomach.

"That was absolutely delicious. My compliments to the chef," she said.

Hunter glanced around the bedroom.

"What's wrong?" she asked.

"I'm searching for the hidden cameras. The way you just mowed through your food, and a good portion of mine, I figured there's some kind of hidden camera in here." He leaned over and peeked under the bed. "Are we taping a reality show I don't know about?"

Ali laughed. "Touché," she said. Then her eyes widened. "Oh my, I certainly hope we weren't being filmed in here today. Though you did give quite the performance."

"Glad it met with your approval."

"I think I made that pretty clear."

Hunter thought about her nails digging into back and the sound of his name on her lips as she moaned with pleasure.

She pushed back the covers, got up, and began picking up her discarded clothes.

"Hey, where do you think you're going?"

"I've already taken up most of your day. It's time I went home."

He reached for her hand and pulled her gently back toward the bed.

"Not yet," he said. "We haven't had a chance to get acquainted."

She arched an eyebrow as she crawled back in bed. "I don't think we can get any more acquainted than we did this afternoon."

Hunter pulled her close, and she settled back, her head on his shoulder. He liked the way she felt in his arms and in his bed. "I know your body." He touched the center of her chest with his forefinger. "Now I want to know you."

Before today he'd held back asking her much about herself because he hadn't wanted to ruin the moments when she'd let her guard down around him. Also, she would have been perfectly within her right to tell him to mind his own business.

However, they'd spent the day sharing the most personal of physical intimacies, and he didn't want to simply leave it at that. He wanted to go deeper.

Hunter felt her shrug. "There's not much to tell. My aunt's school is in financial trouble. She asked me to help, and here I am."

"No, that's your aunt's story," he said. "I want to know more about the woman I just made love to."

Ali stiffened.

Making love with Hunter had been easy. She'd wanted him from the moment she'd seen him, and being with him had been better than she could ever have imagined.

An attentive lover, he'd fulfilled needs she hadn't even known existed before today.

But talking?

The only thing he'd learn was he'd just slept with a big screwup, a woman who had it all and somehow let it slip through her fingers.

"Are you sure you want to talk?"

Ali slipped her hand inside his robe and ran her fingers over the hair on his hard chest. Today had been so wonderful. She didn't want to taint it by talking about herself.

He took her hand and splayed it over his heart.

"You can trust me, Ali." His body was warm,

and his heartbeat was strong and steady beneath her hand.

Ali pulled her head off his shoulder and sat up. She inhaled a deep breath and blew it out.

"I used to have the life Erica wants, not the money, but the rest of it. I was an author with a popular newspaper column, married to a local television weatherman. We were big fish in a little pond," she said. "Our calendar was filled with everything from nightclub and restaurant openings to lavish parties and charity fundraisers. We were the golden couple, always featured in newspapers, magazines, and blogs covering the local south Florida scene."

Ali glanced at Hunter to gauge his reaction, but his face gave nothing away. He hadn't approved of Erica's courting society mavens. What did he think now that she'd admitted to once moving in the same circles?

"So they accepted you even though you weren't wealthy?" Hunter asked.

Ali nodded. "I'm sure part of it was our high-profile careers," she said. "But what I lacked in money, I gave in time. Don't get me wrong—good causes need money. However, they also need people who don't mind doing tons of tedious, drudge work for free."

"Erica never talked about volunteering," Hunter said.

Ali shrugged. "Brian, my ex, never did, but I did enough for the both of us. I chaired fund-raisers for the library, the local ballet, and opera as well as served on at least a dozen non-profit boards."

Hunter shifted on the bed. Turning sideways, he crooked his elbow and rested his head on the palm of his hand. She couldn't help noting he continued to hold her hand fast against his heart.

"So, how did you manage all the volunteering and work too?"

"I ended up hiring a personal assistant to help me stay organized. My best friend, Kay, was looking for work at the time, so it seemed like a natural fit."

Ali paused. She'd lived with how foolish she'd been to believe Kay was her friend, and practically everyone in south Florida knew. Still, it was hard for her to tell Hunter.

He patted her hand, which he still held over his heart. Again, she felt reassured by its steady beat.

"Like any normal couple, Brian and I had our problems. The biggest was I wanted kids, but he wasn't ready. Still, I thought we were okay."

Ali focused on the feel of Hunter's hand on hers as she told him how Brian had lost his job for accidently telling a dirty joke on air. How despite his profuse apologies, he was fired and the only station interested in him after that was a low-power station in rural Wyoming.

"I tried everything to keep his spirits up. I encouraged him to get out and volunteer with me, but he wouldn't. He just sat around the house playing video games like a teenager," she said. "I knew he was depressed. He refused to get help, and I stupidly thought our love would see us through."

Ali cast her eyes downward, the memory of how she'd knocked herself out trying to make Brian happy filling her with renewed humiliation.

She felt Hunter lift her chin with his finger until their gazed locked. "You weren't stupid. It's never stupid to try to help someone you care about," he said. "I didn't realize that until listening to you now."

His meaning wasn't lost on her. He was fresh off a similar ordeal. One he would need time to heal from, she reminded herself.

"Thank you for saying that," she said. "I know you've just—"

He stopped her with a shake of his head. "We've been talking about me ever since I walked into your office. I want to know all about Ali."

She shrugged. "I guess the rest of it unfurls like a Lifetime television drama."

"That's the cable channel where the women are always crying, right?"

Ali paused to think about it a second and then burst into laughter. "I guess their shows do feature a lot of drama and angst, which illustrates my point perfectly."

Ali was grateful for the bit of levity before she

got to the part where everything she'd worked so hard for came crashing down around her.

"Unfortunately, while Brian's career was spiraling downhill, mine was on the upswing. I'd turned in a new book proposal about good manners in bad times. There were talks at the paper about syndicating my column, and there was a local television show in the works."

"Television. Wow, I'm impressed," Hunter said.

"It was supposed to be a midday talk show, where I interviewed local newsmakers about activities and events happening around south Florida."

Confusion registered in Hunter's eyes. "Your husband had a problem with that?" he asked. "I would think he would've been proud of you. I am."

"Actually, he was thrilled. Well, initially. He saw it as an opportunity for him to make a comeback. He wanted my agent to go to the producers with the idea of including him, and we'd do the show as a man and wife team," she said. "I didn't want to, but he was just so despondent. Anyway, my agent broached the topic—"

"Let me guess, they didn't want him," Hunter interrupted. Outwardly, he appeared calm, but she could see sparks of anger in the depths of his dark eyes.

She nodded. "He expected me to turn down the offer. When I wouldn't, things got even worse between us. He moved into the guest room and gave me the silent treatment for weeks at a time."

"Why did you put up with it?"

"By then I was fed up, but filing for divorce felt too much like kicking him when he was down. So I put up with him," she said, matter-of-factly. "Until I came home one day and found him in my bed, screwing my best friend."

Hunter reached over and pulled her into a hug. "I'm sorry, sweetheart."

"He didn't even apologize. He'd done it on purpose. He wanted me to catch them. He said his life was ruined, and he had nothing to lose by ruining mine too."

"If anything, throwing that loser out improved your life."

She shook her head. "He and Kay, who was a good friend of mine before she became my assistant, basically launched a war against me in the local media."

"Nobody believed them, right?"

Ali shrugged. "Separately, his portrayal of me as a power-hungry, emasculating wife would probably have been viewed as messy divorce fodder. However, combined with lies from Kay, it made his story look legitimate," she said. "Kay had the nerve to file a lawsuit against me claiming mental abuse."

"What happened?"

"The judge threw it out, but by then the

damage was already done. The paper backed out of syndicating my column and eventually let me go. And of course, no book or television deal," she said. "Nobody wants a disgraced etiquette expert."

"Damn, I thought I'd been through an ordeal with Erica, but you . . ." He shook his head. "You've been through hell."

Having kept it inside all this time, Ali was surprised what a relief it was to finally get it out. It was as if saying it all aloud had taken the power from anger and bitterness—the soul-stealing emotions that had been eating away at her ever since she'd walked in on her husband and her best friend.

"No, I'm okay now. I'm finally ready to put it behind me."

"You're smart, savvy, and capable. I'm betting you'll have even better things ahead of you careerwise."

Ali abruptly straightened. She looked around the room until her gaze landed on the clock on the nightstand and she saw it was well after nine at night. "Speaking of careers, I have an interview downtown at the newspaper in the morning. I should get home."

She allowed herself one last kiss, before gathering her clothes and putting herself together the best she could. She didn't need a mirror to know she was still a mess.

Hunter was waiting for her downstairs when

she finished. It wasn't fair, she thought, envying his ability to go from bed to gorgeous in a few minutes. He'd slipped on well-worn jeans and a snug black T-shirt that hugged his torso in a way that made her want to drag him back to bed.

Hunter drove her back to the park to retrieve her car and insisted on following her to make sure she made it home safely.

"Good luck at your interview," he said, after walking her to her apartment door.

"Thanks, I'll take all the luck I can get."

He lowered his head until his lips were inches from hers. "Well, allow me to give you a little more."

He brushed his lips against hers in a whisper-soft kiss that took her breath away, and Ali couldn't help wondering if he'd also taken her heart.

Chapter Sixteen

Hunter had been with Ali all day. How could he already miss her? he wondered as he drove in the direction of his town house.

When he'd brought her back to his place, he'd known she was sexy and beautiful. By the time she'd left, he'd also learned she was compassionate, strong, and incredibly resilient.

Somehow the knowledge made what had happened between them today feel like more than just sex.

He was glad he'd decided to go run after he'd left Erica's rather than hole up at his place beating himself up.

Remembering he was supposed to work out with Pete in the morning, Hunter pulled out his cell phone. He'd run over twelve miles today, not including his regular morning run. No way he could run again tomorrow morning.

"Hope I'm not waking you guys," he said when Pete answered.

"Nope. Just catching up on sports highlights.

Sandy's next door at her book club, and I finally got the boys to bed," he said. "What's up?"

Hunter switched on his turn signal and made a right. "Just wanted to let you know I won't be able to make it in the morning," he said. "It's been a long day. I'm sleeping in tomorrow."

Pete chuckled. "You mentioned you were going by Erica's place this morning. Did you end up spending the day on the snob circuit?"

"Nothing like that," Hunter said. He wasn't going to get into it, but he might as well and get the I-told-you-sos over with. "Erica and I are over."

"Good."

Hunter waited a beat, but the I-told-you-so never came; neither did a bunch of intrusive questions.

"You okay? Do you want to stop over for a beer or something? I think Sandy has some of the pie you like in the kitchen."

"I'm okay." Hunter yawned as he turned down his street. "I'm about to pull into my garage. I'm in for the night."

"For what it's worth, I'm sorry things didn't work out the way you'd hoped with Erica, but I can't help but think it's for the best."

Hunter thought about the amazing day he'd spent with Ali and couldn't help agreeing with Pete.

"It feels like the best thing that ever happened to me," he said.

* * *

Ali rolled over and glanced at the clock on her nightstand. The glowing green digital numbers reminded her it was twenty minutes past three in the morning, five minutes since she'd last checked.

After spending the bulk of yesterday making love with Hunter, she'd dropped off to sleep the moment her head hit the pillow.

It didn't last.

Sometime in the night her conscience roared to life like an angry bear, and it hadn't approved of her sexy romp with Hunter.

You shouldn't have kissed him in the first place.

Tossing on her bed, Ali tried defending herself to her perturbed conscience. Hunter had kissed her. It had caught her totally off guard.

Oh, please. He'd just left that awful scene. He didn't know what he was doing.

Ali stared at the ceiling in her darkened bedroom and replayed the kiss in her mind. Could she have mistakened pent-up longing on her part for desire on his?

Hunter was vulnerable and you took advantage.

No, Ali countered. Hunter was the one who'd initiated them taking their relationship to the next level.

He'd just broken up with his girlfriend, for God's sake. You didn't even wait for the body to get cold.

Ali tried rationalizing her behavior. She'd wanted him so badly. She'd tried to walk away, but she couldn't. Images of them in the shower played through her mind, and she sighed. It had been so good.

He needs time. Not sex.

Ali flipped onto her side and pulled the covers over her head. She'd heard enough. She had a big interview tomorrow, and she needed her rest.

It was nearly five in the morning when Ali finally gave up on getting back to sleep. Throwing back the covers, she sat on the side of the bed.

Her conscience had been right. She shouldn't have slept with Hunter.

No matter how good it had been between them, it couldn't happen again. He needed time to heal, and she needed to keep her focus on the school and her career.

Ali walked to the kitchen, flipping on lights along the way. She pulled a microwave egg and cheese sandwich from the freezer and switched on the coffeemaker.

The microwave had breakfast under control. So Ali used the three and a half minutes to retrieve her navy business suit from her closet.

Her interview at the newspaper was in just a few hours. She needed to keep it at the forefront of her mind, not Hunter.

It was shortly before nine in the morning, when Ali followed a security guard through the maze of desks to the managing editor's office of the *Nashville Journal-Gazette*.

Like most newsrooms, it would be at least another hour before it came alive with the low buzz of telephone conversations and the manic clicking of computer keys.

The guard stopped at an open office door on the far side of the newsroom. Ali looked past the guard. A man with a thick head of silver hair was looking intently at the newspaper spread out on his desk.

"Mr. Hicks." The guard knocked on the door. "Ms. Spencer is here."

Ali took a deep breath to steel her nerves, straightened her back, and smiled.

The man behind the desk took off his reading glasses, folded the paper, and put it to the side.

"Come on in." He stood and beckoned her inside the office, before turning to the security guard. "Thanks for bringing her up."

Ali walked into the office. Every inch of wall that wasn't a window held a certificate or an award plaque.

"Impressive," she said.

"I've just been in this business a long time." He shrugged and extended his hand. "Doug Hicks."

She shook it briefly. "Alison Spencer."

He gestured for her to have a seat in a chrome and leather armchair near his desk. His shirt-sleeves were rolled up to his elbows, and Ali could see where his jacket had been carelessly tossed on a pile of papers behind his desk.

"Well, Ms. Spencer, it appears you have friends in high places," he said. "Vivian Cox called me personally and asked that I grant you an audience."

Ali rested her leather tote bag on the floor beside the chair. "I appreciate your agreeing to see me," she said.

"So, how exactly do you know Vivian?" Doug Hicks retrieved a different pair of eyeglasses from a case and leaned back in his chair as he wiped them with a cloth.

"To be honest, I don't. She's a close friend of my aunt's. I had no idea she'd spoken on my behalf until my aunt gave me your card the other day."

"Ahh." He put on the glasses. "Now that you're here, I'll tell you the same thing I told Vivian. We simply don't have a need for an etiquette column. Between the economy and online competition, our paper, like many others across the country, is struggling. I've had to lay off twenty-five percent of our editorial staff over the past year."

"That's exactly why you should hire me," Ali said confidently. She'd known the interview would be an uphill battle, but she also knew she couldn't afford to take no for an answer. "My column at my former paper was quite popular with readers. It increased their reader base as well as attracted advertisers from houseware and department stores. I believe it would do the same for the *Journal-Gazette*."

She leaned over and pulled a copy of her résumé from her tote.

"I don't need this." He dropped the résumé on a stack of papers. "I've already Googled you and read a few of your old columns. I'm familiar with your career and writing style. I also read about your personal problems."

"About my personal problems . . ." Ali was going to explain it was all lies, but he waved her off.

"I'm divorced," he said simply. "Mine was also messy."

Her relief must have been visible, because he continued. "I haven't read your books, but your columns are witty and well written. You somehow managed to hold my interest in a topic I don't have a bit of interest in, if that makes any sense."

"Thank you," Ali said.

"But like I told you, we're barely hanging on, and I'm looking at another round of possible layoffs," he said. "I can't afford an etiquette columnist."

Outwardly, Ali maintained her professionalism, but her insides felt as crumpled as her hopes. She'd been banking on turning this opportunity into a paying job.

"I understand," she said.

She rose from her chair and extended her hand. "I appreciate your time, Mr. Hicks."

"If it's any consolation, if I could, I'd hire you

in a second," he said, shaking her hand briefly. "You're the best applicant I've seen in a long time."

Ali nodded as she retrieved her tote bag, figuring he was simply trying to take the sting out of the rejection. Her mind had already skipped ahead. How was she going to break it to Aunt Rachel that she was fresh out of new ideas, and it looked as though they'd have to close the school after all?

"No, really," the editor said, walking with her toward his office door. "You'd be shocked at how many applicants I've interviewed over the years with no idea how to present themselves."

"What do you mean?" Ali's curiosity was piqued.

"Every year, I get a slew of college graduates who come in for interviews wearing faded jeans and wrinkled shirts that look like they slept in them. Some of the ladies show up wearing dresses appropriate only for strip club auditions."

Ali stopped in her tracks. "You're joking, right?"

"Do I look like I'm joking?"

Ali noted there wasn't a trace of a smile on the managing editor's face. "You'd think a college graduate would know better," she said.

"The poor clothing choices are only part of the problem," he said. "They don't even bother to turn off their cell phones. I've even had them glance down at their e-mail and respond to their text messages *during* an interview."

Ali felt her mouth drop open.

Doug Hicks shrugged. "On paper they have everything going for them, but their first impression . . ." He paused and shook his head. "Purple hair. Weird tattoos. Maybe I'm too old-fashioned, but I can't have them representing the paper."

"I'm stunned," Ali said.

"Don't be. My brother manages a department store and sees the same thing with potential hires. So do a lot of my friends who own their own busin . . ." He stopped midword. "Sorry to go off on a tangent, but the lack of professional savvy I see these days is a sore point with me. I guess I got carried away."

"No need to apologize." Ali smiled to herself as an idea crystallized in her head. "But would you mind directing me to your advertising department?"

Chapter Seventeen

Taj St. John checked his appearance in his car's rearview mirror and straightened the knot of his silk tie.

Tearing himself away from another champagne breakfast atop Erica's high-thread-count sheets had been difficult, but he'd already blown off one day at work to be with her. Although he was his own boss, he couldn't afford to skip work again.

He shut off his car's engine and felt his phone vibrate in the interior pocket of his suit jacket. He checked the incoming phone number and smiled.

"I got your present, baby," a female voice purred.

"Do you like it?" Taj eased back into the seat of his *borrowed* BMW. Work could wait, he thought.

"What girl doesn't love pearls?" She laughed softy, and the sound reminded Taj how much he missed her. "But you shouldn't have."

He knew they'd talked about stashing away cash, but he couldn't resist spoiling her. Besides, if things went according to his plan, he'd be able to shower her with jewelry and give them the life they deserved.

"Did you get the money?"

"Yes, I got it . . ." She hesitated. "But I worry about you. What if . . ."

The concern in her voice touched him, but it also strengthened his resolve to give her everything she could ever want. "Don't worry about that."

"But what if you—"

"I won't." He cut her off, refusing to entertain the thought.

"But—"

"Look, I gotta go. Love you." Taj blew out a sigh as he pressed the button to end the call. Business was too good to quit now.

Besides, it looked as though he'd be due for a fat bonus soon. Compliments of the two prosperous-looking old biddies at Starbucks who couldn't stop raking a woman named Erica Boyd over the coals.

She'd been everything he'd overheard.

Self-absorbed. Shallow. Grasping.

All qualities he'd planned to use to his advantage.

Taj grabbed his briefcase and jumped out of the car. He brushed an imaginary piece of lint from his tailored business suit as he crossed the street.

"Morning, sir." A man carrying a cup of coffee and walking a golden retriever spoke as he passed by.

Taj inclined his head in acknowledgment. It never ceased to surprise him how much respect a well-groomed man in a good suit commanded.

Instant legitimacy. He looked as though he belonged.

Taj paused briefly as if he were checking the house number before strolling right up to the front door of 1079 Christie Street.

There wasn't a house across the street yet, and the recessed doorway made him invisible to the houses beside this one.

Reaching into his briefcase, Taj pulled out his moneymaker. Then he wedged the crowbar between the door and the doorjamb and pulled until he heard the melodious sound of cheap wood splintering.

He hadn't seen an alarm company sign in the yard, nor had he heard one when he pushed open the door.

An alarm wouldn't have stopped him anyway. The cops would undoubtedly head to the more established *Christy Way*. The street he was on, *Christie Street*, was too new to be on a map or register on a GPS. So if there had been an alarm, it would take the cops at least ten minutes to figure out the mix-up.

Thank God for developers who tried to out-skirt city planning regulations on streets with the same name by spelling them differently, Taj thought.

He inhaled deeply as he moved swiftly through the living room to the master bedroom. He'd studied the house's floor plan on the builder's Web site and had committed it to memory.

Like with most of the new constructions he'd visited, the owner had sprung for brand-spanking-new furniture. The place reeked of it.

Once in the bedroom, he glanced longingly at the flat-screen television mounted to the mall. The temptation to pry it off was strong.

"Money and jewelry, money and jewelry," he chanted the reminder as he dumped the contents of a jewelry box onto the bed and began rifling through it.

Junk, he thought, quickly surveying the pile of faux baubles, until a ruby bracelet caught his eye. He pocketed it and moved on to the bureau, tearing through the drawers.

Taj glanced down at his watch, before grab-bing the side of the queen-sized bed's mattress and flipping it over. His eyes lit up when a thick business envelope fell to the floor.

"Cash," he said, peeking inside it. "My favorite."

Taj spent another five minutes in the room,

looking into what most people mistakenly thought were hiding places, taking anything of value that would fit into his briefcase. Then he left the house on Christie Street the same way he had come in, right through the front door.

He looked down the street as he walked back to his car. Opening the trunk, he slid his briefcase into it and pulled out an empty one identical to it.

Taj couldn't help whistling as he drove slowly down the block. He still had work to do along Christie Street.

"I'm going to have to stick you under the dryer for twenty minutes, Miss Boyd."

Erica blew out a sigh. For the life of her, she couldn't understand why a spa day was considered pampering or even remotely relaxing.

She'd spent the afternoon running from room to room of the Babe Salon for a massage, facial, nails, and now hair. She didn't care what anybody said, looking good was hard work.

"Would you like a glass of wine or coffee?" her stylist asked before pulling the dryer hood over her head and switching it on.

Moments later the stylist returned with a glass of white wine in one hand and the latest issue of *Making a Scene* magazine under her arm.

Erica immediately reached for the magazine. The slim, glossy magazine was a free weekly covering social events throughout the county, and it was her habit to thumb through it at the salon while her hair dried.

She studied the cover and frowned. It was a shot of Vivian Cox and her cochair from the Library Ball. She thought about how the woman had practically snatched her donation check from her hands and then proceeded to avoid her the entire evening.

Erica crossed her legs and opened the magazine on her lap. Taj had been her saving grace that night. He'd taken the sting out of her being snubbed by dancing with her and making her laugh. He'd told her how beautiful she'd looked that night in red, and his compliments had made her stand taller.

Hunter hadn't done that for her.

Unlike Taj, Hunter didn't understand she didn't need him getting angry on her behalf or trying to protect her feelings. She needed him to use masculine charm to help her persuade Vivian and the rest of her friends what a terrific asset she'd be to the country club and their Ladies' League.

But she and Hunter were over now. Even if a small piece of her heart didn't want to believe it.

Erica took a sip of her wine. Her leg swung back and forth as she continued to flip through the pages.

A photo caught her eye and she did a double take, her glass nearly slipping from her trembling fingers. She put the wineglass down on the table beside her and looked closer to make sure her eyes weren't playing tricks on her.

It was her, all right. Erica felt her face break out into a huge grin as the stared at the photo of herself dancing with Taj.

ERICA BOYD DANCES THE NIGHT AWAY, the caption underneath it read.

She quickly scanned the page and spotted a second photo of her snuggled up to Taj. She didn't remember posing for it, but that wasn't surprising considering the amount of champagne she'd consumed that evening.

In the close-up photo, they were both smiling and it was obvious to anyone what an attractive couple they made.

SOCIALITE ERICA BOYD AND TAJ ST. JOHN DAZZLE AT LIBRARY BALL, the caption read.

Erica pushed back the dryer hood, picked her purse up off the floor, and began sifting through it for her cell phone. She scrolled through her contacts until she got to her publicist's name.

Carrie answered on the first ring. "I take it you've seen the latest issue of *Making a Scene*," she said.

"Oh yes, and I'm extremely pleased."

"There are a few more photos of you and your date on *Making a Scene's* Web site, Miss Boyd," the publicist said. "I promised you results."

"You already have my schedule, but just to remind you, tonight I'm attending that cocktail

party and benefit concert." Erica couldn't remember exactly what cause it was benefiting,
but that was beside the point. "I expect to see
more of these good results."

Erica snapped her phone closed. However,
before she could stick it back in her bag, it rang.
Taj's name popped up on the tiny screen, and
she smiled.

"Just wanted to hear your voice," he said. His
smooth tones reminded her of melted chocolate.

"How's work going?"

"I'm done for the day, so I'm headed to the
driving range to work on my golf."

Erica was impressed. Golf was a game important deals were made over, and apparently Taj
understood that fact. She spotted her stylist
coming to check her hair and waved her off.

"I've got a little surprise for you tonight," Taj
said.

"Really, what?" Erica asked, unable to keep
the excitement out of her voice.

"Like I said, it's a surprise."

"Well, I'll see you tonight, then."

"My tuxedo is pressed and ready to go."

Erica released a contented sigh. She didn't
have to cajole this man into proper attire or beg
him to attend etiquette classes.

Taj St. John was her ready-made knight in
shining armor.

Chapter Eighteen

"You've got to find whoever did this and get my mother's ruby bracelet back."

A woman with spiked gray hair walked Hunter to her broken front door, which a locksmith was busy repairing and replacing the lock on.

"You will get the bracelet back, won't you?"

He and Pete had already interviewed her, but she continued to ask them the same question over and over since they'd arrived at the scene.

"We'll do our best, ma'am," Hunter said, knowing even when they did catch up with whoever had done this, chances were slim her jewelry would be recovered.

"But you don't understand," she said. "It was the last present my father gave her before he died."

The tears brimming in the woman's eyes spilled down her face. "She only let me take it to get the clasp fixed. She didn't want to," she said. "I was going to give it back to her this evening. How can it be gone?"

Hunter could feel the muscle in the side of his jaw jerk as his back teeth ground against each other. He looked across the woman's porch at Pete, who mirrored his frustration.

They'd been working this case for weeks, and they hadn't got one step closer to finding a suspect, let along apprehending one.

"I hope her mom takes it okay," Pete said, after they were back on the sidewalk.

Hunter shook his head. "Did you hear her say her mother is ninety years old?"

"It's going to break that old lady's heart."

"And we couldn't say a damn thing to soften the blow."

Hunter stood at the end of Christie Street and blew out a long breath. He wondered how many other homeowners on the street would come home to discover they'd been victimized.

He and Pete had investigated two already. All obviously done by the same suspect.

"What's keeping Morrison?" Pete asked. "He should be here by now."

Hunter shrugged. "I'm going to start knocking on some neighbors' doors. Two houses on one block. Somebody had to have seen something," he said.

Pete looked around. "What neighbors?

He was right, of course. Like the rest of the subdivision that had been hit, Honey Bee Glen was new. Only two hundred of the proposed six hundred houses had been built so far, and they were scattered throughout the development.

"I got to do something," Hunter said. "I'm going to start on the street behind this one."

Pete inclined his head in the other direction. "I'll take the one over here. Hopefully, we can turn up a good old-fashioned nosy neighbor."

Hunter's frustration mounted as he stepped off another porch with no more insight than he had before he'd started. It was the same story every door he knocked on. Nobody home, and if they were they hadn't seen anything.

He sighed as he trudged up the driveway of a house a street over. A man opened the door and an eager golden retriever bounded down the drive.

The dog danced around Hunter's feet, until he leaned over and patted him on the head.

"Mike, get back here," the man called.

Mike gave Hunter's hand one last friendly lick before returning to his owner.

"Can I help you?"

"I'm Detective Coleman, Nashville Police Department." Hunter held out his identification.

"I'm investigating the burglaries of at least two of your neighbors' homes today, and I'd like to talk to you."

The man's mouth fell open. "Burglaries? Here? I just moved in a month ago. These are brand-new houses," he said. "You're kidding, right?"

Hunter shook his head. "Unfortunately, no."

"Have a seat, Detective Coleman." He gestured toward two rockers on the porch.

Unlike the homes that had been burglarized, Hunter noted, this elevation didn't feature a recessed entryway.

The man extended his hand. "I'm Art Pryor, and this is my dog, Mike," he said. "Can I get you anything? I have cold beer and soda in the fridge."

Hunter shook his hand briefly. "I'm good, thanks."

"So, you said these burglaries occurred today?"

Hunter nodded as he listened.

"I had the day off, so I've been home all day. I had no idea."

"And you didn't see or hear anything out of the ordinary? Anything or anyone out of place?"

"That's the thing, there's so much construction noise around here. The hammers, drills, and construction vehicles drown everything out," Art said. "As for strangers, I haven't had a chance to meet anyone yet."

It was a familiar refrain, Hunter thought.

"The burglaries occurred one street over from you on Christie Street," Hunter said. "So anything you could tell me would be helpful."

"Yeah, of course. Just ask."

"Were you at home all day?" Hunter asked. "You didn't leave the house at all?"

"Actually, I took Mike for a walk earlier, and we were on Christie," he said.

Hunter's ears perked up. "Can you remember approximately what time?"

"Hmmm." He pressed his lips together. "Shortly after nine in the morning."

"Mr. Pryor, I'd like you to try and remember every person you saw, talked to, or walked by," Hunter said. "Don't leave anyone out."

He shrugged. "I was just out walking the dog, you know? I really didn't see anyone."

"Just think," Hunter pressed.

The man took a deep breath and exhaled.

"Do you think retracing your steps will help jog your memory?" Hunter asked.

"Let's see, I saw a guy on a bulldozer and workers bricking in the house on the corner with the Sold sign out front. And we walked past a thin lady with silver hair as she was backing her car out the driveway."

"Had you seen them before today?"

Art nodded. "I'm pretty sure I have," he said. "Oh, there was also the guy in the suit. I think he was a real estate agent or something."

"Was he wearing a name tag?"

The man shook his head. "I'm not sure."

"Did you see which house he went to?"

"No, I just said hello as we walked past him. I didn't turn back around to look."

It was probably nothing. Still, Hunter made a

note to stop at the model home and get the names of any Realtors who had shown or checked out houses that morning, so he and Pete could talk to them.

"Can you tell me what the guy looked like? Did you happen to see his car?"

"He was tall, with short hair. Maybe black, maybe Hispanic. I couldn't tell. He had on a dark suit, and I think he was carrying a brief-case."

"Would you know him if you saw him again?"

Art nodded. "Probably."

More than likely it was nothing, but it wouldn't hurt to check, Hunter reasoned. Maybe the Realtor had seen or heard something they could use.

"Do you have a number where I can reach you in case I have more questions?" Hunter asked.

The man rattled off his number, and Hunter made note of it. Then he passed on his business card. "If you remember anything else, give me a call."

Ali slowed her car to a stop in front of the familiar two-story Colonial and immediately spotted her aunt kneeling in a bed of sunny daffodils.

Ali had insisted Aunt Rachel take a well-deserved break. No classes were scheduled. So there wasn't a reason for the older woman to spend a gorgeous spring day stuck at the school.

Her aunt, who apparently hadn't heard her car pull up, abandoned her weeding and turned around when Ali closed the driver's-side door.

"Morning, Alison. I was hoping you'd drop by. I've been dying to hear all about your interview," she said as Ali crossed the lawn. "How did it go?"

"Fabulous," Ali said. "In fact, I drove straight here from the newspaper office. I could hardly wait to talk to you."

Ali watched her aunt's smile brighten. "That's wonderful news. We're going to have to find a way to celebrate your new job," she said, yanking off her gardening gloves.

"Oh, I didn't get the job," Ali corrected. "Apparently, the newspaper's finances aren't much better than ours."

"I see." Her aunt's smile faltered. "I'm sorry, dear. I was hoping . . ."

Ali touched her aunt's arm. "It's okay, Auntie."

"I don't understand. If you didn't get the job, why are you so excited?"

"Well, the managing editor of the paper said the most interesting thing. It flipped on the lightbulb inside my head, and I came up with what I think is a great idea."

The older woman picked up her spade and stuffed it, along with her gloves, into a yellow gardening bag. "Let's go inside, and you can tell me what's on your mind."

Ali followed her inside the house both Aunt

Rachel and her father had grown up in as children. Decades ago, her aunt had had her own house, but sold it after her husband died and moved back into the old family house.

"Make yourself comfortable in the parlor while I clean myself up," her aunt said.

Ali took a seat in a chair in front of the bay window with a view of the front yard.

She glanced around the room. The knick-knacks that had covered every surface, when Ali visited as a child, were long gone. So were the huge floral sofa and overstuffed chairs.

Aunt Rachel had decluttered and redecorated the older home, declaring she wasn't going to be one of those old ladies sitting in a pile of junk.

Now the room was a palette of creamy off-white set against gleaming cherry hardwood floors. The only decorations were vases filled with spring blooms and a framed black-and-white photograph of Ali's late uncle.

"Would you like something to drink?" her aunt asked when she returned.

Ali shook her head, and watched her aunt sit in an identical chair across from her. "Now tell me what the editor of the paper said that has you so excited."

"Well, as I was leaving, he noted I was the best job candidate he'd seen in years. He went on to say how he'd interviewed candidates with terrific résumés but who didn't know how to present themselves to potential employers."

Her aunt nodded for her to continue.

"They're coming in rumpled or inappropriate clothing, using slang and their cell phones during the interview."

Ali watched the older woman's eyes widen.

"Not to mention wild hair colors and exposed tattoos with vulgar sayings," Ali continued.

"Are you sure those aren't isolated incidents?" Aunt Rachel asked. "It seems common sense would dictate that kind of behavior is unacceptable for a job interview."

Ali shook her head. "Mr. Hicks mentioned other employers were having the same problem, even with college graduates," she said. "As for it being common sense, maybe to some people. However, there seems to be a sizeable number of people who just don't get it. And I'm sure they're wondering why they're being turned down for jobs they're qualified to do."

Her aunt's smile returned and Ali knew the realization had dawned on her. "So you're proposing we start a class tailored toward job seekers?"

Ali cleared her throat. "Actually, Auntie, it's more than simply a proposal. I immediately took out an ad that begins running in tomorrow's newspaper. It's already up on the *Journal-Gazette's* online edition."

She held her breath waiting for her aunt's reaction. Before now, Ali had been careful to discuss these matters with Aunt Rachel in the form of a suggestion.

"Tell me more," her aunt said.

"The new classes are called 'Get the Job.' One is tailored for people new to the job market. The other is geared toward those who've been unemployed and looking for work."

The older woman appeared to mull Ali's statement over. Finally, she nodded. "I think you're on to something with this idea of yours."

"Really?" Ali straightened in her seat. "So you approve?"

"Yes, of course," her aunt said. "I can't believe we didn't think of it before now. With unemployment at record highs, it is essential job seekers know protocol and how to present themselves in the best light."

"Exactly," Ali agreed.

"Now tell me, what can I do to help get this project off the ground?"

"I thought you'd never ask." Ali reached into her bag and retrieved her notes. She began to lay out the details of the hastily written plan she'd come up with while still at the newspaper's offices.

"I can't tell you how pleased I am," her aunt said. "I'd begun to have my doubts on the significance of a charm school in this day and age. Thank you for showing me we're still relevant."

Ali smiled. "It's like you told me when I was growing up. Good manners will never go out of style."

Her aunt reached over and took her hand. "Your being here has meant the world to me."

Ali squeezed her aunt's hand lightly. "Me too."

Chapter Nineteen

Ali opened the front door to the school.

She was nearly halfway home when she realized she'd left her laptop in her office and had to swing back by the school to retrieve it.

"Excuse me, miss," a voice called out from behind her as she stepped through the door.

Ali turned around to see a florist truck on the curb and a deliveryman bearing a vase filled with at least two dozen deep pink roses approaching.

"Need help with directions?" she asked.

"No, this is the right address. I've been by here twice today, but no one was around," he said. "These are for Ali Spencer."

Giddy with excitement, Ali managed to hold off her curiosity long enough to tip the deliveryman. She placed the vase on the reception desk and opened the card.

"Hope your interview went well," she read aloud. "Dinner tonight at six. Will pick you up at your place, Hunter."

Ali pressed her nose against an open bloom and inhaled its fragrant scent. She held the card to her chest a moment as images of spending the majority of yesterday in Hunter's bed came rushing back.

Unfortunately, so did her conscience.

He needs time. Not sex.

Ali folded the card and slid it into her purse. This time she wouldn't argue with her conscience. Because she cared so much for Hunter, this time she'd heed its call.

"You want to have dinner at our place?" Pete asked. "We're just throwing some steaks on the grill."

Hunter pressed the key remote to unlock the driver's-side door. "Thanks for asking, but I'll pass."

Pete stopped in the middle of the precinct parking lot and stared at him. "Since when do you turn down steak?" he asked. "It's not like you've got a date tonight."

Hunter glanced at his watch. It was a little before five, which gave him just enough time to go home, shower, dress, and make it to Ali's by six. The busy and frustrating day hadn't kept thoughts of her at bay.

He could hardly wait to see her tonight.

"Wait a minute," Pete said, following him. "You do have a date, don't you?"

Hunter gave him a curt nod. "And if I stand

out here gossiping with you like an old lady, I'm going to be late."

"Are you and Erica back together?"

"No." Hunter slid into the driver's-side seat of his car and started the engine. He looked up to see Pete tapping on the window and rolled it down.

"Then who?" Pete asked.

Hunter hesitated. It wasn't as though he was trying to hide anything. Everything was so new with Ali. He wanted them to enjoy this time and each other.

"It's Ali, isn't it?"

Hunter struggled to keep his face unreadable, but he knew he was grinning like an idiot.

"I knew it," Pete said. "I noticed the way you two looked at each other when you thought no one was looking."

"Jeez, you are like an old lady."

Less than an hour later, Hunter stood in front of Ali's apartment door. He couldn't help noting this visit was different from the others and not just because it was at her apartment.

This time when he saw her, he didn't have to struggle with the guilt over his attraction to her or wonder if she felt the same way about him.

Ali opened the door. He stared at her a moment, and his heart did an odd flip-flop in his chest.

"You wore your hair down," he said. "It looks pretty that way."

The corners of her mouth pulled into a slight smile at the compliment as if she hadn't received one in a long time. He'd change that, he thought.

Ali beckoned him inside, and he caught the fresh, citrusy scent of her perfume as he walked past her.

The entryway spilled directly into the living room of the small space. The white walls and beige carpeting were the standard apartment issue, but Hunter was surprised to see Ali's décor had an earthy flair.

Her sofa and matching armchair were in a muted green. There were no tables. Instead, two giant leafy houseplants flanked the sofa, adding drama to the neutral room.

Her taste surprised him. With her penchant for pink, he'd expected her place to brim over with pink and frills.

"I have to admit, this isn't the way I'd expected your place to look," he said.

"I've had so much upheaval in my life lately, I needed my space to have a serene, Zen-like quality. If that makes any sense."

"Yeah, it does. I guess I'm surprised not to see any—"

"Pink," she answered for him. "You haven't seen the bedroom and bathroom yet. Oh, and speaking of pink, I got the roses. They're lovely."

She inclined her head toward the kitchen, where he spotted the roses on the center of the small table.

"One of the reasons I sent them was to wish you luck on your interview. How did it go?"

Ali shrugged. "The interview part went well, but I'm not sure if anything will come of it. Everybody's in a budget crunch these days."

He reached out and touched her arm. "The interview wasn't the only reason I sent the flowers," he said. "I wanted you to know last night was special to me. It had nothing to do with what happened between me and Erica."

He looked directly into her eyes, because he wanted to make sure she understood him. "It was all about me and you."

Ali averted her eyes. "Hunter, I think we should talk."

A lump of dread formed in Hunter's stomach. From her expression and the tone of her voice, he knew he wasn't going to like what she was about to say.

She gestured for him to have a seat on the sofa. However, instead of sitting next to him, she distanced herself by sitting across from him in the armchair.

"Yesterday was special. You have no idea how much being with you meant to me," she began.

Hunter waited for the inevitable "but."

"But we should have waited. You're on the rebound and you need time to get over Erica," she said. "I don't think it's a good idea for us to jump into bed again."

Hunter listened as she went on with what sounded like a speech she'd rehearsed before he'd arrived. Only she had it all wrong. How could he make her understand the only things he felt where Erica was concerned were pity and a great deal of relief?

Her mind was made up, he thought. Nothing he said would convince her otherwise, especially after the job her ex had done on her.

Only his actions would persuade her.

"I'm not here for sex, Ali. I got plenty of the hot sex yesterday, so I'm good."

He watched with a certain amount of satisfaction as her mouth fell open into a stunned O. "I'm here to take you out on our first date."

Hunter rose and checked the time on his wristwatch. "If we're done with this conversation, I think we should get going. I don't want to be late."

Ali bit into the gourmet sandwich and chewed.

She knew the chutney and ham panini with Gruyère cheese she'd ordered was probably delectable. It certainly looked good, and the grill-pressed homemade bread smelled heavenly. But it might as well have been peanut butter on white bread for all she cared.

She glanced across the table of the European-style café in the city's downtown library at Hunter. He seemed oblivious of her agitation. In fact, he dug into his food as if he hadn't a care in the world.

"Is something wrong with your sandwich?" he asked. "You've barely touched it."

Something was wrong all right, but it wasn't the food, Ali thought. She'd expected him to put up some kind of protest when she'd drawn the line on them having sex again.

Instead, he shrugged it off as though it was no big deal. So of course his lack of interest had only piqued hers.

"No, it's great." She took another bite.

And why did he have to look so good? she wondered. He wore khakis and a polo shirt in a shade of brown that made his dark complexion look even richer.

Ali hadn't eaten all day, but if she'd had a choice right now between him and her sandwich, she'd definitely opt for a taste of him.

Hunter eyed her picked-over sandwich again. "Well, if you're done we should walk over to the courtyard. The concert should be starting soon," he said.

As they walked through the main library, Ali couldn't help noticing the marble floors and stone walls of the stately building.

"This looks like a New York City museum," she said. "It's hard to believe it's a library."

"I've been here at least a dozen times, but it never fails to impress me."

She listened as Hunter told her about the

library's lunchtime summer concert series, where the public could enjoy their packed lunch and listen to up-and-coming musicians for free.

"The response was so positive, they occasionally offer a spring or fall concert in the evenings," he said. "Tonight's concert is free too. I hope that doesn't bother you."

Ali looked up at him to find him studying her face. "No, why would it?" she asked.

He shrugged. "I want you to know I brought you here to listen to good music in an elegant but casual atmosphere," he said. "I wasn't going for a cheap date."

"The thought never entered my mind," she said. Honestly, she was just happy being with him. She didn't care how much the date cost.

The spring sun had yet to set when they reached the library's courtyard, and the sounds of musicians warming up and people chatting filled the warm early evening air.

She looked around at the central fountain surrounded by scattered wrought-iron bistro table sets, stone benches, and potted trees. If she didn't know better, she'd think she was in an outdoor Parisian café instead of downtown Nashville. With the tables already filled by couples, she and Hunter sat next to each other on a long stone bench.

"I first heard the Latin quartet playing here this evening at a concert here last summer,"

Hunter said. "They have a good sound. I think you'll enjoy it."

"If their warm-up is any indication, I'm sure I will."

Ali shifted on the stone bench. She told herself she wasn't afraid to touch him, but still was grateful for the inches of space separating their thighs. Her relief was short-lived.

As more people filed in searching for open seats, they were forced to sit closer and closer. Ali swallowed hard. She could feel the warmth radiating off his body and smell his subtle cologne.

They began to play, and Ali prayed the music would be enough to divert her attention from the man seated next to her.

The quartet played the four instruments with enough sound and emotion to fill a concert hall. Nearly half the crowd was now out of their seats. They'd pushed back the tables and chairs and made an impromptu dance floor.

She stole a peek at Hunter, who was tapping his feet in time with the lively music.

"I'd ask you to dance, but I'd only end up stomping all over your feet," he said with a self-deprecating chuckle.

"Your last lesson is dancing, but I guess there's no need for it now," she said.

The sun had set by the time the band finished its last number, and the four musicians took bows to a standing ovation.

"Now I understand why you wanted to hear

them play," Ali said to Hunter as they walked the short blocks to the lot where he'd parked. "I'm definitely a fan."

"That's exactly the way I felt the first time I heard them," he said.

The evening hour enabled them to leave the downtown area without running into any traffic snarls.

"So, tell me more about the new classes you mentioned," Hunter said.

As Ali filled him in on her plans for the school, she couldn't help feeling touched by his interest and enthusiasm for her project.

She stole glances at Hunter while he drove.

"I won't lie," he said. "I'm for anything that keeps you here in Nashville."

Both she and Hunter were quiet as they made the short trek to her apartment door. She wanted to tell Hunter that her sex ban didn't extend to good-night kisses.

Ali was relieved when he pulled her into arms. As he lowered his head, she hotly anticipated his kiss. However, to her disappointment his lips touched her forehead instead.

Thanks for nothing, Ali fumed at her conscience, and wondered why she'd listened to it in the first place.

Taj watched Erica's eyes nearly pop out of her head when he slipped the ruby bracelet around her wrist.

Usually he would have transformed it, like the rest of the jewelry from his last haul, into quick cash. However, he thought he could make better use of this particular gem by using it to fertilize the sapling of his money tree. And he could always steal it a second time.

Taj forced himself to focus on the woman in front of him instead of looking out of her floor-to-ceiling windows at the amazing view of the city at night.

"Oh, Taj. It's gorgeous," she said, her eyes still glued to her wrist.

"I took one look at it and knew it was perfect. The rubies remind me of the red dress you wore the night we met."

She threw her arms around his neck and kissed him hard on the mouth. He tamped down the guilt he felt over his girlfriend sitting at home. This was work, he thought. Besides, she never had to know.

The kiss ended and Erica's attention went back to her new bracelet.

"I've never seen anything like it before. Is it an antique?"

He nodded, though he had no idea. All he knew was the stones were real. "I know we haven't known each other long, but I wanted to give you something to show you how unique and special you are."

"Oh, Taj, this has to be the best gift I've ever received. I'm never going to take if off," she gushed. "But you shouldn't have gone through so much trouble for me."

Don't worry, I didn't, he thought. Aloud he said, "Nothing is too much trouble where you're concerned. And have I told you how lovely you look tonight?"

Taj watched her spin around to show off a dark blue gown that was cut low in the front and in the back, but it was the sapphire and diamond cocktail ring on her hand that got his attention. If only he could find a way to slip it off her finger sometime tonight. It would probably fetch more than he would have gotten for the bracelet.

"Do you think I should change into something red to match my new bracelet?"

Taj shook his head. "Not when you're making blue my new favorite color." He winced inwardly at the sheer corniness of the line, and then looked at Erica, who was eating it up.

"Oh, Taj." She grinned.

Taj glanced at his watch. "We have time for a quick drink before we go?"

"But we're going to a cocktail party."

"There's nothing that says we can't relax with a glass of wine first," he said. The truth of the matter was he was hoping to delay their arrival. The more time they spent at the cocktail party, the better chance of her finding out he was a fake.

She smiled. "I guess a glass of wine would help take the edge off," she said.

"Edge?" He took her hand. "What's wrong?"

Erica shrugged. "It just important to me to make a good impression. I need these people to like me."

He pulled her into a hug and dropped a kiss on the top of her head. "How could you make anything but a great impression?"

An hour later, he was escorting her inside the ballroom of the downtown hotel where he'd mentally prepared himself for the cocktail party, which would be the most difficult part of the evening. Hopefully, the concert would start early.

"Taj, I just spotted the McAdamses. Why don't you introduce me?" Erica asked.

"Are you sure you wouldn't like some champagne first? After all, this is a cocktail party."

"No, I want to meet the McAdamses," she said, annoyance creeping into her tone.

Perspiration broke out on Taj's palms. "The McAdamses?"

"Stop teasing, Taj. You know, Emmett and his wife, Audrey. They own the largest black bank in the region. Some of their customers are your biggest clients."

"Sorry, I didn't mean to tease you."

Taj searched his brain, but the names didn't ring a bell. He'd talked to a lot of people that night, mostly dipping in on strangers' conversations, hoping Erica would take the bait.

"Just lead the way," he said.

He had winged it that night, Taj thought. It looked as if he would have to wing it again.

Taj's nervousness ebbed some as Erica led him directly to the portly, frog-eyed man and woman who looked as if she spent an extraordinary amount of time on the plastic surgeon's table.

He remembered the guy, all right, Taj thought. He'd interrupted an intense conversation between him and another blowhard about golf. The two had acted as though they were discussing the solution to world peace instead of a game.

Taj turned on his pearly whites, grabbed the man's hand, and gave it an enthusiastic shake. "Emmett, it's good to see you," he said, pumping the man's limp hand.

Confusion blanketed Emmett McAdams's features and Taj could see him struggling to place him.

"I caught the first round of the Heritage Tournament. Do you think Briggs will hold his lead?" Taj asked. "I don't care what anybody says, that kid's amazing."

Relief surged through him as Taj watched the man's face go from confusion to a wide smile, and he not only shook Taj's hand, but slapped him on the back.

There was nothing black men of a certain age loved discussing more than African-American golfer Dixon Briggs. Even if they didn't know

PHYLLIS BOURNE

the game, they'd have their televisions tuned
into golf whenever he played in a tournament.

"That so-called slump, or whatever those
know-nothing sportscasters called it, is definitely
over," Emmett McAdams crowed.

Diamonds flashed before Taj's eyes as the
woman with Emmett threw her fingers in the
air. Each one looked as though it was weighed
down with rings.

"Oh no. Not with the golf. Once he gets
started, he can't stop," she said.

That's exactly what I'm counting on, Taj
thought.

"Slump? That was no slump. He was just adjusting his game," Taj said, repeating what he'd
heard Emmett tell one of his friends at the pre-
vious party.

"Exactly," Emmett said, beckoning two more
middle-aged men to join the conversation.

Taj felt a nudge to his side and remembered
Erica. "Oh, Emmett, have you met my date, Erica
Boyd, yet?"

"Nice to meet you," Emmett said. "You've got
you a smart man here, Miss Boyd. You make
sure you listen to him."

"I will," Erica said.

Taj listened to Emmett and his friends talk
golf, adding a comment here and there, until
their wives pulled them away to find their seats
for the concert.

When they were seated, Erica looped her arm through his. "Taj, I'd like to talk to you about advising me on my portfolio," she said.

"Are you sure?" Taj said, trying to sound nonchalant.

Erica nodded. "If Emmett McAdams thinks I should listen to you, then that's good enough for me."

Chapter Twenty

Ali paced the living room of her small apartment. The Zen-like feel she'd tried to cultivate was totally lost on her tonight.

Two days had passed since her date with Hunter, and she missed him like crazy. She stared at her telephone and willed it to ring. When it didn't she picked it up and punched the first two digits of his number.

She put the receiver down.

Stalking off to the refrigerator, she pulled her stash of chocolates from the vegetable crisper. How could she call him after she'd been the one to insist he needed time to heal? Hadn't *she* been the one to say they shouldn't make love again?

Frustrated, Ali peeled the foil wrapper off a chocolate and popped it into her mouth. What would she say to him anyway?

"I know what I said about giving you time to heal, but how about coming over and giving me a little sexual healing?" she mimicked.

So much for taking the high road, she thought.

Damn, conscience.

She ate another piece of candy.

A knock at the door sounded, startling her. Figuring it was someone with the wrong apartment, she peered through the peephole.

Hunter.

Ali closed her eye, and then opened it again to make sure he was really there and it hadn't been just wishful thinking on her part.

It was Hunter, all right, making a simple gray T-shirt and jeans look like *GQ* magazine material. She glanced down at her bare feet, rolled-up jeans, and T-shirt that had seen better days and felt shabby in comparison.

Don't be silly, she scolded. *You're acting like a teenager in love* . . . No, she couldn't be. Ali banished the thought from head.

He knocked again.

She took a deep breath, pasted what she hoped passed for a casual smile on her face, and opened the door.

"Good, you're home."

He smiled and Ali felt her heart do a flip-flop in her chest.

"I wasn't expecting to see you," she said, moving aside to let him in.

"Were you busy?"

Ali shook her head. "No. What's on your mind?"

Part of her longed for him to say he'd stopped by to beg her to put them both out of their misery and reverse her ridiculous "no sex" declaration.

Then she wanted him to sweep her into his arms, carry her into her bedroom, and make love to her until she forgot she'd suggested something so dumb in the first place.

"How are you at painting?" he asked. At her silence, he repeated. "Painting," he said, slower. "As in helping me paint a dining room."

Ali frowned, getting out of her daydream. "But your place looks new. Why would you want to paint it?"

"I'm painting the dining room of the house I inherited from my grandma," he said.

"Oh, that's right. I do remember you mentioning it," Ali said. "You recently finished remodeling the kitchen, right?"

Hunter nodded. "So, can you give me a hand?"

Ali shrugged. It wasn't exactly her fantasy, but it was better than scarfing down chocolates thinking about him. "Sure. Just give me a moment to find a cap."

Minutes later, they were in Hunter's car headed across town.

"Are you hungry? We can stop and get something," Hunter offered.

"No, I already ate, but . . ." Ali hesitated. She wasn't quite sure how to approach the subject.

"What?" Hunter glanced at her briefly, before returning his attention to the road.

"I just wanted to ask how you've been. I know the scene with Erica was rough, and it's only been a few days."

Hunter shrugged. "I'm good. I was angry at myself, mostly for not following my gut and breaking it off with her months ago."

Ali touched a hand to his shoulder. "You don't have to downplay it on my account," she said. "I've been there. I know what you're going through and it's hard."

Hunter surprised her by pulling over to the side of the road. He tapped on the steering wheel with his fingertips, before turning to her.

"Excuse me, Ali. I know you mean well, but our situations are totally different. You were in a marriage," he said. "I was committed to someone who disappeared a while ago. My love vanished along with the old Erica. I stayed out of some misguided attempt to protect someone I cared about from herself."

"I didn't mean to—" Ali started.

"If you want to know what hurts, here it goes. It hurts to want you and not be able to touch you." He brushed his knuckles against her cheek, sending a rush of heat to her core. "What's rough is now that I'm free to be with you, I have to wait until you believe that it's you I really want."

Taken aback, Ali turned to face him. He

leaned across the armrest and brushed his lips against hers in a gentle kiss. Though it was brief in contact, its tenderness rocked her world.

God help her, she *was* in love.

Painting?

Hell, he didn't need any help painting. He'd cleaned, patched, repaired, remodeled, and restored the entire kitchen himself. He'd even turned down his own father's offer of help.

So why did he want to bring Ali here?

Hunter unlocked the door to the house and turned on the lights. He still didn't have an answer to the question. Although he'd only known her a short while, being with her felt as natural as breathing.

Taking her by the hand, he couldn't help noticing how adorable she looked with rolled-up jeans, her hair tucked under a baseball cap, and a slick of pink gloss on her sweet lips.

His gaze lingered on her mouth. Just one taste, he thought as he pulled her to him.

Hunter felt her arms slip around his neck as his lips descended on hers. He should have known a simple taste wouldn't be enough. He slipped his tongue between her lips and heard her moan deep in her throat. Her cap slipped off her head, and he sank his fingers into her silky hair as it spilled onto her shoulders.

She felt so soft in his arms, her body melting into his like a second skin.

When the kiss ended, Ali still clung to him.

"I believe we were headed to the kitchen," she said breathlessly.

Hunter nuzzled her neck as he willed his pulse to return to a normal rate. God help him, she smelled as good as she tasted.

He dropped his arms to his sides, reluctantly releasing her from his embrace. "The kitchen is right in here."

He led the way. Though the last place he wanted to take her was the kitchen. He wished he were taking her back to his place and upstairs to his bed, where she belonged.

But it would just have to wait until she believed in the growing feelings between them and that she was indeed the woman he wanted.

Hunter watched a look of awe cross Ali's face as she took in the white-on-white décor. The house had been built in the 1920s and the kitchen was miniscule by today's standards. So he'd thought the white would open it up.

"It's beautiful," Ali said, smoothing her hand over the exposed brick, which he'd also painted white.

"You don't think the white's too impractical," he said.

She shook her head. "Not at all. It makes it seem huge, and though those windows are small it looks like it's brimming over with light."

Ali crouched down and touched the

indentations of the penny-tile floor. "I love the unfussyness of it, if that makes any sense."

"It's exactly what I was going for," he said. "My grandma wasn't a fussy woman. Although she's gone, I wanted the place to still be a reflection of her."

Ali nodded. "I think she'd be proud."

"I'd like to think so," he said, feeling the familiar pinch of guilt.

"So, are you planning to move in here when you finish remodeling?"

Hunter shook his head. "No."

"Why not?" Ali asked. "You've put so much hard work just into the kitchen alone. Don't get me wrong, your town house is nice, but this place has so much character. It feels like a home."

Hunter shrugged and walked back toward the dining room. He felt Ali's hand on his arm. "What did I say?"

"It's not you. It's just . . ."

"Just what?"

Hunter shook his head. He didn't want to get into this with his father and he didn't bring Ali here to get into it with her.

"Well, the dining room isn't going to paint itself," he said.

"The painting can wait."

Hunter turned to find Ali with both hands planted firmly on her hips. "Nothing's wrong, Ali," he reiterated, but she didn't move.

He walked back to the threshold separating the dining room and the kitchen. He took her hand, raised it to his lips, and kissed it. "I told you, there's nothing wrong."

She placed her hands on his chest and raised her gaze until it met his. "Like you told me the other night," she said, "I want to know more about the person I made love to."

"You already know me."

She tapped the spot over his heart. "Tell me more about your grandma and this house," she said. "And why it's so important to you to make it just right."

Hunter sighed. "Okay," he said. "Come sit on the back porch with me."

He led her by the hand back through the kitchen and out the back door. The sun had set and the lack of moonlight made the stars glitter like diamonds against the inky night.

He sat down on the top step. Ali took a seat on the one below it and rested the back of her head against his chest.

"This backyard is huge," she said. "Did you used to play back here?"

Hunter nodded. "And work. Grandma and I planted that row of evergreen trees separating her backyard from the neighbor's. She thought it would look better than a privacy fence. Not that they offered much privacy then. They were barely two feet tall, but look at them now."

Ali tilted her head up toward the top of the eight-foot trees.

"I like it out here," she said.

"I used to love it here too," Hunter said wistfully.

"What happened to change that?"

Hunter felt his shoulders sag as he sighed. "I was in my senior year of college and had just got home for Christmas break. I walked through the door, tossed my dirty laundry to my mom, and was ready to hang out with my friends. We'd all gone to different universities and had plans to meet up for some party."

Ali leaned her head back and looked up at him. "I remember those days. Only my father usually had tons of his laundry waiting on me when I got home," she said.

"Well, my father asked me to stop by and check on my grandmother. She'd missed me a lot and always looked forward to my breaks," he said. "But I blew it off to go party. When I went by the next morning, I found her dead. She'd had a heart attack in her sleep."

He felt Ali's body stiffen and she pivoted around to face him.

"You can't possibly blame yourself or feel guilty about that," she said.

Hunter averted his gaze. "If I had come here instead of partying, I might have been able to revive her."

"Maybe. Then again, maybe not."

"I still feel like I let her down," he said.

Ali turned and leaned back into his chest. "I think you let her down if you're sad every time you think of her, and you continue to define what seemed like a wonderful relationship by one lapse," she said. "I think you'd let her down if you continue to let this beautiful home sit empty. Either you move in or sell to a new family to build a foundation of happy memories."

Hunter kissed the top of Ali's head, his mind flickering briefly to images of them living here together. And sitting on this back porch together at night after they put their children to bed.

Children.

Where had that come from? he wondered, shaking off the errant thought. "Let's go paint."

Chapter Twenty-one

Taj couldn't believe it. Instead of gleefully anticipating getting his hands on Erica's money soon, he was sitting in his car arguing with his girlfriend.

He rubbed the edge of his temples with one hand and held his cell phone to his ear with the other. The more he tried to reason with his girlfriend, the angrier she became.

"Well, explain it to me, then." His girlfriend's shriek was a painful reminder of the champagne he'd overindulged in last night. "Tell me why I'm looking at a photo of you hugged up with some bony, rich bitch?"

"I told you already, it was just work. Where did you get it anyway?"

"My cousin e-mailed it to me, but what does that have to do with anything?" she asked.

The voice that usually purred in his ear bounced off one side of his skull and slammed against the other. "Can we talk about this another time? I'm late for work."

"We can talk about it now. You don't punch a time clock, you rob houses and they aren't going anywhere."

No, Taj thought. He did more than simply rob houses. He'd come up with a foolproof plan that practically turned burglary into a white-collar crime. He didn't even get his suit wrinkled.

Plus, the cops never knew what subdivision he was going to hit until he was already gone.

"So, why aren't you saying anything? Are you with her now?"

"I'm not with anyone but you."

"You still haven't answered my question, where are you?"

"As soon as you stop interrogating me, I'm headed to the Knightsbridge Subdivision to make us some money."

"I tried to call you three times last night, and you never returned my calls."

Taj exhaled sharply. "My battery ran down. How many times do I have to tell you that?"

Ten minutes later, Taj realized he was repeating the same words and getting nowhere with her. He glanced at his watch again. "We'll discuss this later when you calm down. I have to go to work."

"Don't you dare hang—"

Taj powered the phone down and tossed it in the car's glove box. He hoped he'd come across something sparkly this morning to appease her.

*   *   *

Hunter tossed a paper sack on Pete's desk.

Spending time with Ali last night had put him in a good mood this morning. So he'd picked up Pete's favorite breakfast when he'd stopped for coffee, on the way to the work.

"Thanks, man." Pete dug into the bag and pulled out the blueberry muffin. He took a huge bite and rolled his eyes heavenward.

Hunter stopped short as he caught sight of the magazine laid open on his desk. Photos of a beaming Erica and the man he'd caught her with smiled up at him.

He picked up the magazine. The hairs on the back of Hunter's neck prickled, just as they had the first time he'd encountered Erica's new man. His eyes narrowed as he stared at the photos and then looked up at Pete.

"Don't look at me. I didn't do it. It was there when I got here." Pete devoured the last of the muffin and licked the crumbs from his fingers. "My guess is it was Bishop. He always reads that rag."

Hunter shook his head. "Take a look," he said, handing Pete the magazine.

Pete looked at the photographs. "It's Erica hugged up with some guy," he said. "Taj St. John. Never heard of him."

"Look closer," Hunter said.

Pete shrugged. "What am I supposed to be looking at?"

"Check out the pin on the lapel of the guy's jacket."

Hunter stood by as Pete examined the magazine photos. "It's a fleur-de-lis," Hunter said. "One of our victims listed a fleur-de-lis lapel pin as part of the property stolen from her home, remember?"

Pete nodded. "It's probably just a coincidence. There has to be tons of pins like those."

Hunter stroked his chin with his hand. American flag pins were common, but not this one. "I've got a hunch this is our guy."

Pete sighed. "Are you sure your hunch isn't about this St. John character being with Erica?"

"Even if that were true, and it's not," Hunter began, "when has a hunch of mine ever been wrong?"

Both Hunter and Pete knew the answer to that question. So far, Hunter's hunches had been dead-on.

"I'll check to see if the records management system has anything on St. John," Pete said.

Sitting down at his desk, Hunter pulled *Making a Scene*'s Web site up on his computer screen. He clicked his way to the photos of Erica and St. John and then picked up his phone.

"Mr. Pryor, Detective Coleman calling."

"Oh yeah, I remember you from the other day. Unfortunately, I haven't seen anything suspicious yet," Art Pryor said. "So I can't tell you any more than I did last time we talked."

"Do you have Internet access where you are?" Hunter asked, not sure if he had called a house or a cell phone.

"Yeah," Pryor replied. "I'm at work, so I'm sitting at the computer now."

"Give me your e-mail address. I have a Web site I want you to take a look at." Hunter sent the link to the pictures and waited for Pryor to retrieve the e-mail.

"Hey, this is the guy I told you about. I saw him on Christie Street when I was out walking Mike," Pryor said.

"The man standing next to the woman in the red dress," Hunter confirmed.

"Yeah, him. Only he was wearing a suit, not a tuxedo, when I saw him, but that's definitely the same guy."

Hunter looked up at Pete, who was standing by his desk.

"Taj St. John, if that's his real name, doesn't have any outstanding warrants or an arrest record," Pete said.

"It's him. This St. John character is our guy," Hunter said. He began to fill Pete in on his conversation with Art Pryor, but was interrupted by the precinct's administrative assistant.

"There's a woman on the phone who says she has a tip on the burglaries," she said. "You guys want to take it?"

Pete rolled his eyes, and again, Hunter couldn't blame him. Ever since they'd made an appeal to the public for help, they'd received plenty of calls. None of them had turned up anything remotely helpful.

"Okay, put her through to me," Hunter said.

"Detective Coleman here."

The corners of Hunter's mouth pulled into a smile as he listened to the angry woman's tirade.

"Please, ma'am, don't hang up," he said, trying to keep her on the line. "Can I at least get your name and a contact number?"

"I told you where he is. Now you just deliver the damn message."

Left with the dial tone, Hunter hung up the phone and turned to Pete.

"Did she know anything?" Pete asked.

Hunter rose from his seat. "Let's go check out Gray Street in the Knightsbridge Subdivision," he said. "I think there's a well-dressed man over there who pissed off the wrong woman."

Erica popped into Hunter's mind. He had to warn her. He retrieved his cell phone from his jacket pocket as he and Pete dashed out to the precinct parking lot.

The phone just rang at her penthouse. When she didn't answer her cell phone, Hunter left a message for her to call him immediately.

"You okay?" Pete asked as he slid into the passenger side of the Chevy Malibu.

Hunter nodded. "I'll be okay when we catch up to St. John."

* * *

Ali hung up the phone, surprised that it didn't start ringing again.

She released a sigh when it remained blessedly silent. The response to the newspaper ads had been overwhelming. She and her aunt had been fielding calls from potential students all morning.

Both classes were full and there was already a waiting list.

Ali heard a light tap on her open door and looked up to see her aunt in the doorway.

"Sorry I couldn't talk when you popped into my office earlier, but the phone hasn't stopped ringing."

"That's an understatement." Ali chuckled and beckoned her aunt inside. "I think we should consider an additional set of classes to accommodate more students."

"Great minds think alike. I was going to suggest the same thing to you." Her aunt slid a pink message slip across Ali's desk. "Oh, by the way, your agent called when you were on the other phone line. He said it was important."

Ali picked up the paper and shrugged. Leo was probably just doing some housekeeping and wanted to let her know he was dropping her from his roster, she thought.

Her aunt glanced up at the clock, which showed the approaching noon hour. "You have any plans for lunch?"

"Why? Are you cooking?"

"Unless you want to spend the afternoon in the emergency room, no," her aunt said. "I was thinking more along the lines of going out for Chinese. You know that place I like across town."

"Sounds good. I'll grab my car keys."

When they returned from lunch, Ali dropped her purse on her desk and the pink message slip fell to the floor. She picked it up and stared at it a moment.

"Might as well get it over with," she muttered.

Her agent answered on the first ring.

"Great news, Ali," he said.

It had been so long since Leo had sounded this happy to talk to her, Ali nearly didn't recognize his voice. She picked up a catalog on her desk and began thumbing through it.

"What's going on, Leo?"

"Channel Four called. They changed their minds, they want to go through with the television show."

Ali abandoned the catalog. "You're joking, right?"

"Nope, they want you down here ASAP," he said. "How soon can you get a flight?"

Dozens of questions paraded through her mind as her brain scrambled to process the fact that she'd actually gotten the television show.

After being dragged down to rock bottom, she was finally on her way back up.

"Are you still there?" Leo asked.

"I'm here. I'm still in shock," Ali said. "What happened, Leo? What made them change their minds?"

"Their host was arrested in some big drug bust down here. Real sleazy stuff," he said. "They want to revamp the show and stick you in as host."

"Wow, this is all happening so fast," she said.

"I got them to go up twenty percent on their original offer, and they've already faxed over the contracts," Leo said. "All we're waiting on is your signature and you."

Ali got her agent off the phone with a promise to call him when her plane landed in West Palm Beach.

Excited, she immediately scrolled through her cell phone contacts until she located Hunter's name. She could hardly wait to share her news.

"Hunter, my agent—"

He cut her off. "I'll have to call you back, sweetheart," he said. "See you tonight."

That's just it, Ali thought. If she could snag a last-minute flight to West Palm Beach, she wouldn't be here tonight.

The conversation with Leo danced in Ali's head as she walked down the hallway to her aunt's office.

She'd left Florida unemployed and humiliated, but it looked as if she was going to return with a bang.

Ali paused in front of her aunt's open door. Her mouth dropped when she saw Aunt Rachel focused on the screen of the laptop Ali had given her months ago.

"What's going on here, Auntie?"

Her aunt looked up at her and smiled. Ali couldn't help noticing the sparkle in the older woman's eyes.

"It's time I joined the twenty-first century," her aunt said. "Who knows? I may even get myself an iPod."

Guilt warred with excitement as Ali remembered why she'd come to her aunt's office. Her gaze wandered to the portraits of her great-grandmothers on the wall, and her mouth fell open in surprise.

Her photo hung on the wall next to her aunt Rachel. It was the one from the jacket of her last book.

"I had a picture of you enlarged and framed," her aunt said. "I wanted to surprise you."

Ali sucked in a breath.

"What is it, dear?" her aunt asked. "You're not upset about my adding you to the Spencer wall, are you?"

Ali shook her head. "No, it's just . . . It makes what I have to say even harder . . ." She paused. "The call from my agent earlier, it wasn't to drop me."

Her aunt's smile faded.

"The deal for the television show is back on the table. They want me to come down there tomorrow."

The older woman closed the lid on the laptop. "Oh. Well, that's wonderful news for you." Her aunt's voice held a note of cheerfulness, but the light in her eyes had visibly dimmed.

"Yes, it's exactly what I'd hoped for," Ali said hesitantly. But somehow it didn't quite feel like it anymore, she thought.

"So, when are you leaving?"

Ali spoke over the lump lodged in her throat. "My flight leaves tonight. I meet with my agent and representatives from the television station in the morning."

"Well, good luck."

"Auntie, I know we had big plans for the school, but . . ." Ali's voice trailed off.

Her aunt rose from her chair and walked around her desk. Then she surprised Ali by wrapping her arms around her and pulling her into a hug.

"This is your life, Alison," her aunt said. "You have to do whatever you feel will bring you the most happiness and fulfillment."

Chapter Twenty-two

Taj donned his gloves, slid the crowbar between the door and the doorjamb of the second house on his Knightsbridge Subdivision hit list, and listened for the crack of splintering wood.

Either the wood was getting cheaper or his job was getting easier, he thought. Not that he'd have to do this much longer.

He was due at Erica's this evening to talk about his handling her finances. He'd been prepared to put off the Knightsbridge Subdivision for another day, but she had some luncheon scheduled.

Taj could hear the rumble of cement mixers and the continuous beat of a jackhammer from the construction crew a few houses down as he walked through the dining room, which still smelled of fresh paint and new carpeting.

"Typical," he muttered, looking at the showroom-fresh furniture. What was it about new houses that made people insist on cramming them with brand-new furniture and the biggest televisions they could find? he wondered.

Deciding to shake up his usual routine, Taj stopped by the home office first. He took a seat in the big leather chair behind a massive desk and set his briefcase down beside him.

He tugged on the top middle drawer.

Locked.

Taj started to go for his crowbar, but hesitated. He opened the top, side drawer and, sure enough, keys.

Again, typical and so predictable, Taj thought.

The second key he tried opened the drawer and his eyes fell upon a gold Rolex. He immediately took the Movado he was wearing off his arm and slipped on the Rolex, which was definitely a keeper.

By the time he'd finished in the office and cleaned out the bedroom, his briefcase was bulging with cash, jewelry, and a laptop computer.

He smiled to himself as he walked to the front door. He wondered how much this briefcase would weigh once he filled it with cash from Erica Boyd's bank accounts.

Taj opened the door, stepped out on the porch, and froze. The flashing blue lights of squad cars greeted him, accompanied by at least a dozen officers with guns pointed squarely at him.

How?

The word reverberated through his mind as

he dropped the bulging briefcase and stumbled down the porch steps with his hands up, complying with their barked orders. His plan was perfect, Taj thought, as he lay spread-eagle on the ground in his designer suit with his nose pressed against the concrete.

How could they have figured it out?

A big, burly cop in plainclothes handcuffed him, informing him of his rights as he yanked him to his feet.

Taj looked up—directly into the face of Erica's ex.

"How did you figure it out?" he asked, the question burning inside him.

Taj staggered as Erica's ex grabbed the front of his jacket. He braced himself for the punch he was certain to come. The guy had looked as though he wanted to kill him back at Erica's penthouse.

Instead the cop's face broke into a smile, and he pointed at the stolen pin on Taj's lapel. "This pin and a very angry woman you apparently hung up on earlier led us right to you," he said.

Emerging from her bubble bath, Erica wrapped herself in a thick bath sheet.

She was glad Taj left early this morning. She wanted to be on point when she faced the Ladies' Lunch League membership committee this afternoon. She'd even shut off both her house and cell phones so she wouldn't be disturbed. She needed to be mentally prepared for her meeting with the committee.

Erica walked into her bedroom to take another look at the peach linen suit she'd laid out on the bed. She ran her trembling fingers across the smooth silk of the matching blouse and tried not to let her nerves get the best of her.

After all, she'd been quite generous to a lot of the members' pet causes. Yet she still lacked Vivian Cox's endorsement, she thought.

Every time she'd managed to corner the woman, Vivian somehow changed the subject or slipped away.

"Well, you'll just have to make an impression on the rest of them," she said, slathering on a dollop of scented body cream.

After all, she had been making inroads lately. She and Taj had made *Making a Scene* magazine, and she looked forward to seeing photos of them from last night in the next issue.

No, she didn't feel the same way about Taj as she had felt about Hunter. However, with Taj at her side, she was close to getting the recognition she deserved.

Erica exchanged the towel for her dressing gown, and sat down at her vanity to apply her makeup.

When she was dressed, she reached into her handbag for her cell phone. She powered it on to see if she'd received any calls from Taj or the Ladies' Lunch League.

The phone chirped several times, and Erica looked down at the tiny screen. Twenty-seven messages. What on earth was going on?

Carrie's number flashed on the screen as the phone buzzed in Erica's hand.

"Miss Boyd, I've been trying to reach you for over an hour," her publicist said breathlessly.

Erica blew out a sharp breath. "Carrie, can this possibly wait? I have a very important meeting with the membership committee of the Ladies' Lunch League this afternoon."

"Fine," Carrie snapped.

Erica pulled the phone away from her ear a moment and glared at it, not caring for Carrie's tone.

"So, what do you want me to tell the reporters calling about you?"

"What?" Erica asked.

"You mean you don't know?" Carrie asked.

"Know what?"

"Turn on the news, Miss Boyd. Now!"

Erica scurried around the bedroom to find the remote control and turned on the television.

Images of Hunter and Pete filled the screen. Erica plopped down on the bed in stunned silence when she saw they were leading a hand-cuffed and disheveled Taj to a police car.

Taj's mug shot filled the screen and then

came photos of Taj and her together at the Library Ball.

She turned up the television.

"A little over an hour ago, a man police have dubbed the 'Dapper Bandit' was arrested while burglarizing a Nashville home. Taj St. John has confessed to over forty burglaries across the city."

"Miss Boyd, are you still there?" Carrie asked.

Erica continued to stare openmouthed as more photos of her and Taj filled the screen.

"Here's the 'Dapper Bandit' looking quite cozy with girlfriend Erica Boyd," the reporter said. "And this next photo of the two of them was taken just last night."

The anchorman chimed in. "News Channel Thirteen tried to reach Miss Boyd, but she was unavailable for comment."

Erica turned off the television and tossed the phone across the room. She curled up on her bed, not caring if she wrinkled her linen suit.

After all, she no longer had anywhere to wear it.

Taj St. John had surrendered his tailored suit for an orange jumpsuit when Hunter and Pete left the jail. He'd been charged with over forty counts of burglary with more charges to follow.

"Bishop and Morrison are saving seats for us over at Big Johnny's. You're coming over, right?" Pete asked.

Hunter shook his head. "No, you go ahead. There's something I have to do first."

Twenty minutes later, he was on the elevator with Dan riding up to the penthouse level of Erica's building.

"It's a good thing I didn't bet on that basketball game last night. I would have lost big time on that one," Dan said.

"You're right. Nobody expected that team to win," Hunter said absently. "Have you seen Erica at all today?"

Dan shook his head. "No, but I finally had to call the cops to get those reporters out of here after a few of them tried to sneak past me."

"Thanks for looking out for her," Hunter said.

The elevator chime sounded as the doors opened on the top floor. "Just doing my job," Dan said.

Hunter stepped off the elevator and walked to Erica's door. He'd thought he'd feel some lingering anger and resentment over what had happened the last time he'd come to her door, but he didn't feel either.

All he felt was pity mixed with concern for an old friend.

Hunter knocked on the door. When he didn't get an answer, he tried again louder.

"Erica, it's me," he said.

He heard some shuffling noises on the other side of the door. Somebody was there. He knocked again.

"Go away," Erica said.

"I'm not going anywhere until I see for my-self that you're okay."

Finally, he heard the lock turn and the door opened. Erica was barefoot and dressed in a wrinkled peach suit. Dried tears made tracks down her face, and her smudged makeup made her eyes looked as though they'd been blackened.

She ran her hand over her tangled mass of hair.

"So now you've seen me. Are you happy now or do you need to gloat?" She walked over to the sofa and plopped down. "Go ahead."

Hunter sighed. He walked through the door and closed it behind him. "Of course, I'm not happy to see you like this," he said. "And I'm not here to gloat. You know me better than that."

"Then why did you come?"

He crossed the room and stood in front of her. It hadn't occurred to him to gloat. From the looks of her, she'd felt bad enough. She didn't need him piling it on.

"Because we used to be friends," he said. "And I thought you could use one right now."

She sniffed and swiped at tears. "You're my only friend," she said. "The only people who've tried to contact me today are reporters and people scrambling to uninvite me to their parties."

Hunter walked over to her powder room and

retrieved a box of tissues. He handed it to her and sat on the couch beside her.

"It's not the end of the world. St. John will be in the news for another day or two, and then those reporters will forget about you in their rush to move on to a new story."

She blew her nose. "Maybe the reporters will forget, but I'll never get into the country club or the Ladies' Lunch League."

Hunter sighed. "Would that really be so bad?"

"But I've worked so hard. I should have known Taj was too good to be true."

Hunter shrugged and shook his head.

"I know you never approved of what I was doing, but it seemed like I was finally . . ." she continued.

"The big reason I didn't like it is that all it did was make you miserable," Hunter said. "You're smart, beautiful, and have more money than you can spend. I guess I didn't understand, and I still don't, why you let a bunch of strangers determine your self-worth."

Erica blew her nose again, and then stared up at him. "You still think I'm beautiful?" she asked.

He glanced up at her hair, which resembled Medusa's headful of snakes. "Yeah, you look just fine."

"Hunter, I'm so sorry about that scene you walked in on with Taj. I swear I never cheated on you before that." Erica hesitated a moment. "Can you ever forgive me?"

"I already have," he said, honestly.

No, he hadn't been unfaithful, but he hadn't been fair to Erica either. He'd battled his growing feelings for Ali long before he'd found Erica with Taj. Forgiving her was the least he could do.

Erica put her hand on top of his. "Do you think we could ever go back?"

Hunter shook his head. "No, I don't."

Erica patted his hand, before pulling hers back. She left the room for moment, and when she returned she held out the ruby bracelet.

"Taj gave me this, and I doubt he bought it," she said. "Please make sure it gets back to its rightful owner."

Having done what he'd come for, Hunter stood and headed for the door. Erica was down, but she'd definitely rebound.

He drove past the sports bar with every intention of stopping, but he'd celebrate the "Dapper Bandit's" arrest with the guys another time.

Right now, the only person he wanted to see was Ali.

Chapter Twenty-three

Ali tried to ignore the emotional tug of war between her head and her heart as she zipped her suitcase closed.

After all, she'd been hoping for an opportunity like this for months. She'd be a fool to turn it down.

Images of her aunt trying to figure out that laptop came to mind, and Ali found herself smiling as she remembered her aunt vowing not to touch it.

She was grateful when her cell phone rang. She hoped the caller would get her out of her own head. She glanced down at the small screen and saw Hunter's name.

"I stopped by the school looking for you, but no one was there." A delicious shiver shimmied down her back at the sound of his deep voice. "Are you at home?"

"Yes, but—"

"Good," he interrupted. "We just wrapped up a big case, and all I want to do is see you."

If it were possible for a woman to simply melt, she'd be a pool of pudding. She wanted to see him too, badly.

Then her gaze fell on her suitcase.

"Hunter, I can't see you tonight," she said.

She heard him exhale sharply. "This isn't about you still thinking I'm hung up on Erica, is it?"

"No, it's not that. I'm about to drive to the airport," she said. "My agent called, and the television station in Florida has reinstated their offer. I'm meeting with them tomorrow."

"Oh," he said, sounding deflated. "I'm not too far from your place. Can I give you a lift to the airport?"

"Thanks, I'd appreciate it."

Ali pulled her suitcase off the bed, rolled it into the living room, and placed her tote beside it. She'd packed light, but it wasn't as though she was headed to a strange place or a hotel. She was going home.

Although she was expecting him, Ali jumped when she heard Hunter knock. She opened the door and he immediately pulled her into a hug.

She rested her head on his wall of a chest, reveling in the feel of his strong arms around her. Hunter dropped a kiss on top of her head.

"Congratulations," he said.

"Thank you," she said, reluctantly letting him go. "And congratulations to you too, on your case."

He glanced over at her suitcase. "Is that all?"

She nodded.

"Wow, I thought you'd have a lot more than that," he said.

Ali shrugged. "I don't know how long I'm staying, but I have a closet full of clothes at my condo."

"Yeah, I guess you're really just going home, huh?" His voice sounded as though he was trying to infuse it with a cheerfulness he didn't feel.

"Hunter, I . . ." she started, but wasn't quite sure how to finish.

He picked up her suitcase. "We'd better get going. You don't want to miss your flight."

She and Hunter filled the short ride from her apartment to the airport with small talk. Hunter talked about his case and his visit with Erica.

"I'm glad you went to see her," Ali said, feeling genuinely sorry for Erica. "I don't have to work hard to imagine how quickly her society friends turned their backs on her."

"She seemed a bit better when I left," Hunter said.

Ali noted how matter-of-fact he sounded. Maybe he really was over Erica after all.

Hunter parked the car in the hourly lot and walked with her to the terminal. Ali fisted her hand and kept it at her side to keep from reaching out and holding his.

Deep down, she longed to tell him how she felt about him, but what would be the point? She was leaving, after all.

"Don't you have to check in?" he asked when he saw the kiosk for her airline.

"I printed my boarding pass already. Since I only have a carry-on bag, I can go right to security."

She saw his Adam's apple bob in his throat as he swallowed. Ask me to stay, she thought.

Ali looked at the security checkpoint line and back at Hunter. "I guess I'd better go ahead through," she said.

She stood on her tiptoes and kissed him lightly on the lips.

Ask me to stay.

The thought echoed in her mind as she turned around and walked toward security.

"Ali," he called out, and her heart slammed against her chest.

Yes! Ali turned around, fully prepared to leap into his arms.

"I just wanted you to know how proud I am of you," he said.

"Oh," she said, trying to hide her disappointment. "Thank you, that means a lot."

Hunter watched Ali until she walked down the long corridor and out of sight. It took every ounce of willpower he could summon not to go after her.

It had taken even more to let her go in the first place. When she'd kissed him it had been all he could do not to toss her over his shoulder and take her back to his town house, to his bed, where she belonged.

Slowly, he turned around and headed back to the parking garage. As badly as he'd wanted to stop her, he couldn't.

Her ex-husband had ruined this opportunity for her once. How could he ask her not to take it and live with himself?

Instead, he'd told her how proud he was of her. It was true. He'd only wished . . .

Hunter shrugged off the thought. It didn't matter what he wished now. He slid into the driver's seat of his car and inhaled the lingering scent of Ali's citrusy perfume.

He felt a tug deep down in the region of his heart and realized he'd let the woman he loved get away.

Ali awoke with a start as her plane made a bumpy landing at Palm Beach International Airport. She stared out the small window at the night sky as the plane rolled to the terminal.

She was home.

Ali waited for the wave of emotion she would have expected to accompany the thought, but it had yet to make an appearance. She didn't feel it when she saw the palm trees swaying in the balmy breeze on the airport property or the gecko that darted across her path on her way to the rental car parking lot.

She might be back in south Florida, but she'd

left her heart in Nashville, she realized. The feelings she'd forced back when she'd told Hunter good-bye threatened to surface.

"You've got to put him out of your mind. This job is what you've been waiting on," she whispered as she drove south on I-95 toward her Boca Raton condo. She'd be more excited in the morning when she met with Leo and the producers from Channel Four, Ali reasoned.

It was nearly eleven when she reached the front door of her place. She disarmed her security system with her key fob remote before unlocking the door.

Ali flipped on the light, dropped her suitcase in the foyer, and walked around. Except for a layer of dust, the three-bedroom condo was exactly the way she'd left it four months ago.

She opened the sliding glass door to let in some fresh air and took another look at the once-familiar surroundings. The rooms were done in a style her decorator had described as classic luxe.

Now it just seemed crowded and overdone. She took in the Persian rugs, her collection of crystal figurines, and the oversized lithographs hanging on the walls.

Though her tiny apartment in Nashville was less than half the size, it seemed so much more spacious.

Ali thought about Hunter and how he'd expected her apartment to be infused with pink like her wardrobe. What would he think of this place? she wondered.

Then she began to wonder what he was doing now. Was he stretched out on that big bed of his thinking about her?

Maybe she would just call . . .

She instantly vetoed the idea. Parting at the airport had been hard enough.

Besides, the only thing she should be concerned about now was getting a good night's sleep so she'd be at her best tomorrow.

The next morning Ali awoke hours before the sun bathed her condo in light. After tossing and turning half the night, she'd finally gone into her home office and begun preparing for this morning's meeting. She'd located her detailed notes, which were chock-full of segment and story ideas for the show.

As the time for her to meet everyone over at the station drew near, Ali pulled a soft pink shift dress from her closet with a matching short-sleeve jacket.

Fortunately, she'd left enough coffee beans in the freezer to grind and brew a decent half pot of coffee before jumping in the rental car and driving over to the station.

Leo was pacing in front of the station door when she arrived. "Ali, what happened? I thought you were going to call me last night when you

got in, and when I couldn't get in touch with
you this morning, I was worried you were still
in Nashville," he said.

It had been too late to call when she'd arrived, and she'd been too busy to talk on the
phone this morning. "As you can see, I made it
just fine," she said.

"You look great. It's good to see you again,"
Leo said. "This is what we've been waiting for.
You must be thrilled."

Thrilled? Not really, Ali thought. And her
lack of emotion bothered her. Leo was right; she
had been waiting for something like this to happen.

Still, reviewing her old notes this morning
had ratcheted up her enthusiasm. Once they
started talking about the show, she was sure, she'd
feel more excited.

Once everyone was seated in the conference
room with coffee and a platter of donuts, the
producers began to review the format of
the show.

Ali was disappointed to learn both the producer and the director Ali had talked to last
time had moved on to other stations. Now their
replacements were going over their vision for
the midday show.

"We're going to continue to call it *The Town's
Talking* and it will fill the half-hour slot between
local news and the beginning of network pro-
gramming," Jeff, the new producer, said.

He appeared to be in his twenties and fresh out of college. His attention was divided between their conversation and the BlackBerry and iPhone in front of him. "The show will continue to have a talk show, news magazine feel. You'll interview local celebrities and news makers, do stories on events and activities, and host segments on diets, fashion, cooking, and decorating. Our audience is mostly stay-at-home women and seniors, so we want to do topics that appeal to them."

Leo grinned at Ali. "Sounds like this show is just perfect for Ali," he said. Though Ali doubted he'd even been listening. If she knew Leo, his ears wouldn't perk up until they started talking money.

"We think so," the director agreed. She was so young, it made Ali feel practically elderly. Her red hair was scraped back in a high ponytail, and she wore glittery lip gloss that looked as if she'd gotten it with her last Barbie doll. "Ali's background in etiquette will give the show the softer, gentile feel we're aiming for, especially after that horrible business with our last host."

Ali cleared her throat. "I had some ideas for show segments on personal finance—"

"Oh, definitely," Jeff interrupted. "I already have a guest lined up to talk about boosting your grocery store savings with coupon clipping and another one to talk about the best cell phone deals."

Ali nodded. "Those are good ideas, but I was thinking along the lines of recession-proofing your portfolio, avoiding excessive bank fees, and which insurances you really need."

Jeff shot the director a look. "Ali, those are all worthy topics, but they're a little heavy for the afternoon."

"We'd like to increase the recipe segments to two a show," the director chirped. "Who doesn't love recipes?"

"I also have some ideas on simple fixes you can do in your home that would save you tons of money. I can demonstrate those myself," Ali said.

The director looked at her. "How are you with tablescapes, you know, decorating your dining room table with a theme?"

Ali's other ideas were met with similar conde-scending reaction.

"I'll tell you what. Why don't you just send me a memo or something, and we'll keep those in mind? Your input is very important to us," Jeff said.

"Ali will certainly do that," Leo said. "She wants to do everything she can to ensure that the show is a success."

Leo, Jeff, and the director continued to talk as if she weren't in the room. And as their voices prattled on in the background, Ali realized why she hadn't been as excited as she should have been about this job.

That was it—it was just another job.

Other people would have the decision-making authority as well as the power to get rid of her anytime.

She wanted more than just a job. She realized she wanted something of her own.

"Excuse me." Ali interrupted the conversation about her future she'd been all but excluded from. "I appreciate your consideration and your generous offer, but I'm going to have to pass on it."

"What?" Leo sputtered, jumping to his feet.

"I don't want the job," Ali said.

"You can't be serious," Leo said.

Jeff looked over at the director. "Get that lady who bakes the cartoon cakes on the line. Offer *her* the job."

Ali walked out of the studio into the bright south Florida sunshine, and for the first time since she'd arrived she felt excited. She could hardly wait to go home, back to the school, to her aunt, and to Hunter.

Chapter Twenty-four

Hunter turned down both Pete's offer of dinner and Bishop's, who had an extra ticket to a Nashville Sounds baseball game.

He knew he'd be poor company tonight, and it was no use ruining everybody else's evening. All he wanted to do was get in his car and go home.

You should have asked her to stay.

The thought had echoed through his head ever since he'd said good-bye to Ali last night. How could he have let her go without telling her he loved her?

He already knew the answer. He could never ask her to turn down the opportunity she'd already lost once for him. That would make him no better than her ex-husband.

Hunter knew now, as he had known last night at the airport, he had to love her enough to let her go.

He turned down the street that led to the Spencer School. He rationalized he was only going that way to get coffee at the nearby shop, not because he already missed her like crazy. The fact that tonight would have been his last lesson wasn't lost on him.

Just as he signaled to make the right turn into the coffeehouse parking lot, Hunter thought he saw Ali's red Honda parked in front of the school.

No, it couldn't be, he thought.

He abruptly braked, causing the driver behind him to honk his horn.

Hunter told himself not to get his hopes up. It could be that her aunt had simply borrowed the car. However, his heart felt as if it were about to leap out of his chest.

He parked his car, jumped out of it, and ran to the door of the school. Closing his eyes briefly, he took a deep breath before pulling the door handle.

Relief mixed with joy flooded him when he saw her standing by the reception desk rifling through her tote. She looked up and smiled brightly. "Hunter," she said. "I was just about to drive over to your place."

"Why are you back here so soon? I thought you'd be down in Florida getting ready to launch the television show."

She shook her head. "I turned it down."

"What?" Hunter asked incredulously. "I don't understand. You'd been waiting for that opportunity to open up again. It was your dream job."

Ali shook her head. "No, I had it all wrong. It was just a job. Somebody else's job that they can fill on a whim," she said. "My new dreams are here with this school and with—"

Hunter rounded the reception desk and pulled her into his arms. "With me," he finished for her.

She nodded. "Yes, with you."

Hunter raised her chin with his finger and lowered his mouth to her. His kissed her until they both had no choice but to come up for air. He wanted there to be no doubt in her head that she was the woman he wanted.

"So, you never did say why you came by the school," she said.

"I believe you owe me a dance lesson."

She smiled. "But first, I think we need to talk about reversing my no-sex policy."

"How about we head back to the airport and catch the next flight to Las Vegas?" he asked. "Then we can reverse it on our honeymoon."

Made in the USA
San Bernardino, CA
11 December 2016